BORDER
MARKERS

A NOVEL

JENNY FERGUSON

Library and Archives Canada Cataloguing in Publication

Ferguson, Jenny, 1985-, author
Border markers / Jenny Ferguson.

(Nunatak first fiction series ; no. 45)
Issued in print and electronic formats.
ISBN 978-1-926455-69-3 (paperback).--ISBN 978-1-926455-70-9 (epub).--
ISBN 978-1-926455-71-6 (mobi)

I. Title. II. Series: Nunatak first fiction ; no. 45

PS8611.E7379B67 2016   C813'.6   C2016-901687-0   C2016-901688-9

Board Editor: Anne Nothof
Cover design & typesetting: Kate Hargreaves (CorusKate Design)
Original cover photograph: "Darlene, Lisa, Mike, Michael, Ruth, and Jimmy"
by michchap, www.flickr.com/photos/michchap
(Creative Commons Attribution 2.0: creativecommons.org/licenses/by/2.0)
Author photo: Holly Teresa Baker

NeWest Press acknowledges the support of the Canada Council for the Arts, the
Alberta Foundation for the Arts, and the Edmonton Arts Council for support of our
publishing program. This project is funded in part by the Government of Canada.

201, 8540 – 109 Street
Edmonton, AB T6G 1E6
NeWest Press   780.432.9427
www.newestpress.com

No bison were harmed in the making of this book.

PRINTED AND BOUND IN CANADA

I I I I

I I I I

For my family (of course),
and in memory of Dylan McGillis,
whose story was too short.

THE STORY OF THE NEW BUMPER

R UNNING LATE. Cruising along on empty, the light flashing, that warning gong making itself known as Mike attempted to minimize the visual impact of his bald patch in the rear-view mirror by tilting his head in increments. On the passenger seat lay a sad looking bouquet of grocery store checkout flowers, heavy on the limp, little white ones. He drove to that little store, half diner, half grocery store at lunch, out in Lashburn today. That's why his tank hadn't lasted the week. An unintentional trip. The red sticker caught Mike's eye and he thought about peeling it from the Cellophane. Changed his mind as he shifted lanes, accelerating. It might be best if she saw he'd spent a few dollars thinking about her today.

The gas station was coming up on the left. If he didn't turn in, he'd wind up late for work tomorrow. He'd be late for the morning meeting, would miss those minutes when everyone was busy and he could flirt with the new redhead, the secretary, transferred from out east, when he could take a shit in the bathroom on the second floor before the employees working there showed up and wanted to spend twenty minutes in the bathroom taking a shit of their own. So Mike turned into the gas station, reached out to keep his coffee mug from falling from the too-small cup holder, like he did every time he turned left.

One empty spot. Only one on account of the afternoon price drop.

Mike went for it, driving a bit too fast around the corner. He'd have to back in, but it would get him home quicker, to work on time in the a.m. A red dually truck, its bulky wheels heading towards Mike's spot. Trying to take it from him. "Not going to happen, buddy. Never going to happen. Wait your own turn, asshole." He whipped around the second corner with a wicked squeal.

The dually stopped when Mike took the corner. Gave in to Mike, backed off. Time to go for the brake, but during that last left turn, Mike had forgotten to hold a hand out to steady the coffee mug and it came up out of the too-small holder, fell to the floor, rolled under the brake. Mike jumped the curb and hit the pump. A hiss escaped from the pump. The woman at the pump ahead of Mike dropped her gas cap and ran for the road, her arms flailing above her.

Mike felt around the passenger seat for his cellphone, mangling the flowers when they got in his way. He hit the speed-dial. "Yeah, I've got a problem. At the Esso just east of Lloydminster." He took a breath, his hand shaking as he reached for a cigarette. The people around him still standing at their pumps, admiring the truck and damage from a distance, began yelling. "Yeah. An accident," Mike replied into the phone, flicking at his lighter.

❚ ❚ ❚

FRANK ARRIVED BEFORE THE POLICE and fire trucks, so he'd been around, or speeding. His tanned forearm hung out from the window of his tow truck. "This is the second gas station in a matter of twenty kilometres you've got reason to avoid. Ain't it?"

"Shouldn't you be at my wife's party?"

"Shouldn't you be at your wife's party?"

"I don't want to go anymore. With the truck and all."

"Barb'll be disappointed."

"Not the first time," Mike said.

"You better hope the coppers take you in. She might be forgiving that way."

Mike waited on a strip of grass between the gas station and the sidewalk chain-smoking. A few bystanders lingered on, but most drifted back to their own troubles, to the cheap gasoline at the pumps. Someone had a camera. Flashing lights. Mike prayed like he'd never prayed before that they would take him in for the night. Would be best.

8

BLEACHING THE STAINS AWAY

BARB HAD SHRIVELLED BURGERS and dogs on the barbeque though the propane was off now. A few limp streamers hung off the railings of the deck, dangling down into her yard, where her sister's dog was happy to play with the remains. Her hair had fallen as limp as the streamers under the unusually oppressive summer heat. The guests had gone, everyone but Patricia who was in the basement trying to work a wine stain out of her expensive blouse. Barb was pouring the opened bottles over the banister onto her lilacs one at a time. No one would know she'd watered them with wine. The wine was close in colour to the flowers.

Frank rang the house phone while the party was still getting off the ground, said something about an accident, an arrest. For a minute, Barb thought Frank was someone else and that he was calling about Poppy. Barb wasn't sure why. She'd known Frank longer than she'd known her own husband, had never confused Frank for another before. Besides, if some government official were calling about Poppy, he'd speak with a Spanish accent. Or he'd be speaking Spanish. At least last she'd heard, a postcard postmarked Peru: "Don't bother to write, we won't be in this village long enough for a letter to catch up. The post is caught in mudslides most days on account of the rain in any case." But in her heart of hearts Barb was fairly sure that the authorities wouldn't bother calling if Poppy were in trouble; they'd just lock her daughter up and throw away the key. And as far as Barb could figure, Poppy wouldn't care a damn if that was how things ended for her.

Now Barb's husband was in jail. A motor vehicle violation. Endangering public safety. Smoking within ten metres of a petrol station, even when repeatedly asked to put out his cigarette.

And all this on the night of his birthday party. A party she'd been planning for months. If Poppy were here, Barb thought, she'd say something about not wasting good food. Since she wasn't here, a barbeque full of meat, a used-to-be-white patio table with hors d'oeuvres from Safeway, and bottles of Mike's favorite beer were all that remained, with no guests left to eat and drink and help Mike blow out the candles of his cake. And an ice cream cake melting into a congealed puddle on the deck that would stain the wood pink for months.

If Chuck were around... There was no thinking of that. If Barb fell too deeply into that one, she would end up kneeling under her lilacs trying to suck the wine off the leaves.

Patricia called from the door leading from the kitchen out onto the deck, "Where do you keep the Javex?"

"I'm coming. I'm coming," Barb said. "Can't you do anything?"

"Don't get mad at me because your husband is a fuck-up."

"He's... I'm not... We don't call it Javex here. It's bleach."

Putting an arm over her sister's shoulder, Patricia asked, "You heard from Chuck recently?"

Barb inhaled quickly to keep the tears from coming down. "Last time he talked to Poppy, he told her if any of us try to visit he won't see us. It'll be a waste of gas, that's what she said he said!" Then the tears slipped out when Barb wasn't looking. "Both my son and husband. I tell you, it's that neither of them—what am I saying—none of them want to be here."

Patricia pushed her hands into her pockets. "The Javex, Barb?"

"Right, right," she said, wiping the tears with the sleeve of her shirt. "The bleach. What was I thinking?"

WHAT REMAINS

SERGEANT W. LEROY DROVE up to the Esso with his lights flashing, but the siren off. He surveyed the scene from the cab of his cruiser, ensured that nothing was about to explode by catching the eyes of the firefighters standing next to their truck and sharing a professional nod. Only after he had adjusted his cap did Leroy make his way over to the truck parked too close to the pump, ready to figure out what the heck had gone on here. The truck's front tire was shredded by the metal protective barrier wrapped around the number six pump.

"You want what?" Leroy asked slowly, a second time, standing adjacent to the scene of the accident since the fire department had cleared it, staring at the driver.

"I want you to arrest me." Mike leaned against the damaged pump. "Please."

"It doesn't normally go like this," Leroy noted, turning to Frank as if for assistance.

"I can't go home."

"He can't go home," Frank added. Both men were still smoking cigarettes.

"We don't have very nice sleeping quarters, Mr. Lansing. Won't be too comfortable."

"Please."

"I don't want to formally arrest you. Too much paperwork. But I guess… Okay."

"Thank you," Mike said, most sincerely. He offered Leroy a cigarette.

At the cop shop, Leroy brought a pot of coffee and two mugs to his desk. "No cream, sorry," he said. "Sugar's in the kitchen, but I like it black."

"Black's just fine." Mike pointed to a framed photo of a smiling, brown-haired woman. She was holding a bouquet of wildflowers, no little white ones in sight. "Your wife?"

"Late wife."

"I'm sorry—"

"Not you that should be sorry. It happened a while ago."

After a short pause, Mike couldn't help himself from prying. "Were you born here, Sergeant?"

"We moved here to raise the kids. Never did end up having them, the cancer and all."

Mike poured himself a cup of coffee, burnt his lip trying to drink it too quickly. He always did things too quickly, didn't wait in anticipation for the thing to come to him. "Ever think about leaving?"

"All the time."

"Me too. Never have though. All these long years."

Mike watched the Sergeant's face. He wasn't an old man, not yet. But he had lines deep in his forehead.

"Funny how we never met before, the both of us living here."

Mike took another gulp of coffee, could feel the liquid against his lip again, a little less sharply now. "You know one of mine. Arrested him a few years back."

"Charles Lansing?"

"We tried hard with that one, Barb and me. My wife. Never seemed to get through to him."

"Sometimes, Mike, if I'm honest, I'm relieved we never had kids."

The two men shared a laugh in the empty room.

"You should go somewhere," Mike said. "Get away."

They were quiet, pretending to be involved in drinking the still too hot coffee.

"Can't," Leroy said. "Her bones are here."

The graveyard where Leroy buried his wife all those years ago, where Mike had only been once to see his daughter bury her high school boyfriend, was out of town, next to the access road leading to the golf course. Mike travelled down that road often. So did Leroy. Both of them on their way to play a round with friends.

LENDING LIBRARY

THE EDMONTON PUBLIC LIBRARY discarded their too worn for regular service books on the steps of the federal prison once a year in May, a form of routine spring cleaning. That's what they did with the ones without covers, the ones missing a chapter or two, the books covered in layers of multi-coloured highlighter that had leaked through the pages. They also donated books nobody bothered to take out. *Grooming Tips For Dog-Owners* and *Olympic Water Polo: Techniques from the Masters* had found their way onto the prison book cart, care of Edmonton taxpayer dollars and some librarian culling the collection with a sense of humour.

Chuck didn't used to read. The last library he'd been to was with Bill in the basement of the city hall building. Chuck was sure that he'd never stepped one foot into the library at his high school. There was no reason to be there in Chuck's mind. Now, the library on wheels was one of the highlights of his week.

"What are you looking for?" Rickie asked from the comfort of his welded metal bunk. His voice was consistently strained as if there was something wrong with his voice box, something a little deformed. Rickie said it was nothing, normal, no story at all.

"Just take the one with the babe on the cover and let the cart move down the line," Orson, the guard pushing the cart said, his tone curt. It was Sunday. Most libraries were closed on Sundays. Not here.

Chuck answered both men patiently, "I'm looking for something worth reading. Something with a little intelligence."

"Lansing, you're a snob," Orson said. He selected a book and handed it through the bars with a click of his tongue like he was chastising a child or a horse that would not jump. "Take it, or leave it."

"*Critical Theory Since Plato?*"

"You complaining?"

"Nah, I'll take it. Probably won't understand six words in a row, though," Chuck said. "Get myself smart while I'm locked up."

"You think you're getting out?" Orson asked. He got behind the cart and began to push it down the hall toward the next cell, not waiting for a reply.

"Thirty-six days after my forty-third birthday, I will be. Maybe earlier if—"

"Kid killers don't stay out long. That's if they get out at all. That's if they leave this place alive. The other cons don't like kid killers."

"Thanks for the encouragement." Since Orson knew Chuck from back home, he used that knowledge to mediate the uncomfortable feeling settling into the phlegm in his throat.

"Don't thank me. Read your book, asshole."

Yep, Chuck thought when he flipped the book open to the title page: Donated Care of the Edmonton Public Library Systems of Greater Edmonton. Their motto: Learning Through Reading. The spine hadn't yet been broken.

"You actually gonna read that?" Rickie asked. He sat up on his bunk, swung his feet over the edge.

Chuck opened the book somewhere near the middle and creased the spine, enjoying the feeling of the crack. Then he tossed it onto his bed. "What's the point, eh, Rick?"

"We could play some cards? I got my hands on that Marilyn Monroe deck you've been hearing so much about. But it's only in my possession for a week before I'm contractually obligated to return it."

"I'll play anything but Crazy Eights."

"It's the only one I know," Rickie said, shuffling the deck with precision. "Besides poker, and you've got nothing left to lose to me."

Chuck walked to the bars to look down the hall at Orson

and the book cart moving on down the line. It would be a week before he saw those books again. Sunday. There wouldn't be anything different about next time either. Just another Sunday.

THE DEAD

P OPPY LIKED THE FEELING of her sunglasses sitting tight and high on her nose. She walked along the stone-lined path in the graveyard with a scarf that she had let Juan-Aarón buy for her from the market earlier tied up in her hair. This graveyard was nothing like what she knew from back home. No sunburnt grass, no bunches of dead flowers piled next to drab, grey stones. Not a single creepy plastic angel holding a battery powered candle between her praying hands so that the dead would never be in the dark. Those angels, they were always girls, and this struck Poppy as something she was happy to be far away from.

This impromptu tourist excursion, a sidetrack from their planned walk into the countryside, was nothing like what her body remembered: leaning down, the grass biting her bare knees as she placed cheap carnations on a grave too fresh to have a stone to mark his place. Instead compact mausoleums painted in turquoise, yellow and salmon covered the hill. Each one had a little laneway, leading up to a braided metal gate with a keyhole, the kind an antique key with a long neck would open.

"Is it not the nicest final resting place?" Juan-Aarón asked. "Do you like it? Families housed for eternity together."

"Better than most I've seen."

"Do you believe in ghosts?" He took Poppy's hand.

"Yes."

He smiled. One side of his mouth rose higher than the other due to a hardly noticeable scar running through his upper lip.

"So do I. My, ah, mother she is with me always," he said, placing his free hand on his heart dramatically. "Perpetually."

They stopped in front of a mausoleum with a tarnished gate and the family name inscribed in the stone archway. The gate was locked. Inside Poppy could see porcelain vases topping flat stones on the floor, a plush teddy bear, old and well-made.

"I saw my grandfather the night he died," Poppy said as the sun slid behind one of the clouds beginning to form. The rain was coming. "He came to see me. I was just a kid, sleeping on the couch in my basement on a school night, the television playing late night infomercials for some kitchen appliances that you only needed one hand to operate. I remember him looking at me, looking at him. I think my dad bought a jar-opener from the TV after I told him that."

Juan-Aarón raised his eyebrows as he nodded. "Yes. Yes, I have heard of such things. I very much wish my mother would come to me."

"No you don't," she said. "The other one, a high-school-aged boy my brother killed, he follows me. He creeps after me. It's not nice."

Juan-Aarón laughed. "You are kidding me, Poppy! No?" He dragged the "o" out unnaturally.

"I'm kidding, yes." She dropped his hand to move closer to the mausoleum. Poppy lifted her sunglasses to the top of her head. Inside, in the shadows, next to the patriarch's gravestone, she could see the boy's wispy, dull blond hair, covering what she knew were slightly puppy-like ears. She could smell familiar aftershave mixed with the dust.

She waved, this slight movement, was her acknowledgement, her little hello, her welcome back. She wondered if he spent time stalking her brother too.

Juan-Aarón placed a hand on Poppy's shoulder, and was happy when she didn't brush his hand away. He smiled in the graveyard, feeling a touch of Catholic guilt.

A BAD SEED

THREE YEARS TOO OLD for the twelfth grade but Chuck had been taking his time. Step by step. Slowly but surely. At his own pace, as his mother liked to say when long-distance family asked on the yearly phone call. And unprompted, she told the grocery store checkout clerk as she bagged cans of tomato soup and carrots with the green tops still on that her son was on his way this time. Paper, not plastic for the Lansings. Chuck's mother used to say that those carrot tops were good for making pesto. She said that every time she bought the carrots with the tops still on, even though they were more expensive than the bulk bagged kind. Then she never got around to making pesto, and the wilted tops always ended up in the too-full trashcan. And Chuck always got an earful if his dad found the trash overflowing under the sink when it was Chuck's week to empty it, but never when it was one of the girls' turn.

When people asked him about his future plans, he repeated his mother's phrases. Now Chuck was in his sister Poppy's class and things were going good. He had a part-time job that kept him in the money, he was back living with his parents, that meant he was out from under his cousin's thumb where he had been living after the fight, and he figured he would be graduating in the spring. Chuck would wear a smart suit, a flower, sprayed with hairspray to keep it from wilting, tucked in a buttonhole during the graduation Mass.

And Chuck had friends. They were mostly Poppy's friends, but they didn't mind him, would sometimes hang out with him even if Poppy was busy doing homework or working at the pizza place down the road. Friends like Bill.

Bill was short for his age, but he swore he'd grow a foot or two once he left town. Bill had wispy blond hair and faintly puppy-like features, ears and feet a bit too big for his frame, but he was considered attractive. He was always dating someone and lately that someone had been Poppy. Spinning tales of the towns he would live in and the park benches he would sleep on all through his South American sojourn, Bill was always talking about life after graduation and that made Chuck want it even more.

Then again, not everyone was happy with Chuck maybe graduating in the spring. "It's bad for business," his boss had said on more than one occasion. "We got to keep someone reliable in the Catholic school."

Someone to sell the kids pot from his locker before Christian Ethics class, someone who wasn't clutching the rosary too tightly, specifically someone who didn't have to sit in a car in the last row of the student parking lot, the engine running, so he didn't freeze to death during the prairie's tedious winter months. For the last year, that someone had been Chuck. With him maybe graduating, Chuck's boss would have to look for someone else. Someone on the same slow path to success. Like Jimmy Carlson's brother. Or one of the scrappy teenagers whose names were exchanged between mall cops in the break room. Then again, there wasn't much of a point in worrying about the future when Chuck was doing a fine job now and maybe he wouldn't be receiving a diploma in June. Maybe he would only be buying his sister roses and sitting in the audience watching the procession. There was plenty of time to mess things up real fine still.

So that was what Chuck did. The way a stroke victim learned how to walk again, he thought. Each shaky step was leading him towards a goal. One step at a time. Right to where he was at that moment, convicted of killing a friend. That was Chuck's story as Chuck saw it.

He turned over in his bed, the bruise on his hip, dull but still present. Was it Sunday yet? He turned his mom's phrases over in his mind like a balm. One day at a time. Slowly but surely. Like a tortoise moving forward, inch by inch, at a reliable pace.

ANNIVERSARIES

AWOMAN IN PINK SCRUBS pushed her cart up and down aisle six and for the life of her she couldn't remember what she was supposed to buy. It was quarter after seven in the morning, she had just finished a shift from hell where she hadn't stopped to sit and sip her coffee all night, but she had to drop in at the Safeway to get groceries for her son's birthday celebration at school. Was it peanut butter for the cookies he liked? No. Not since all the fuss over allergies had they let peanuts in the schools. Or a box of ready-bake brownies that came with a sleeve of icing and star shaped sprinkles? Something easy so she could pay the babysitter, send her son off to school, throw it in the oven and then get some sleep before—

She stopped in front of the icing sugar and let her eyes fall closed, fall heavily closed for a full half minute. Standing there, clenching the handle of the cart, she could see the bulkier boy handing her a packet of white powder, his hand shaking. The other boy, the one seizing on the stretcher, foaming at the mouth, eyes rolled back in his head so only the bloodied whites showed, continued to seize despite the medications. She had the curtains pulled around the boy for privacy's sake. No one witnessed the bulkier boy, the one not ODing on the stretcher, pass her the evidence. And the information that might help to save the sick boy.

She said, "You did good, kid. This will help."

The bulkier boy slid down the wall and sat on the floor beside the stretcher. When they moved the sick boy upstairs, the other boy followed him, sat on the floor for the next three

21

days. Every time Erin came back on shift, she would take a minute or two to check up on the boys. Not sure which one she was checking up on.

Then the next night, someone told her that he died. "Had a massive seizure. Mira up on ICU said after that the other kid got up and left the room. He said to Mira, 'I guess God didn't want me to walk away from this one. Nobody can fight God when he's made his mind up.' And then, she said, he took off out of the unit."

I I I I

ERIN HAD HERSELF A FEW DAYS OFF in a row after that. She baked a zucchini-carrot cake for her son's birthday. She called her sister in Edmonton and talked about coming for a visit sometime soon when she could afford it. Painted the canvas in the basement that had been half-finished since her son was born. In the bathtub late one night, Erin tucked herself underwater while she cried, concentrating on the sound of the running tap.

The next day, she answered the door with a paintbrush tucked behind her ear, her son laughing at something on cable in the background. The dead boy's parents were pressing charges. Erin told the officer at her doorstep about the white packet the bulkier boy gave her, even though she didn't want to; it had already been recorded on the chart and if she didn't tell, she could find herself in trouble.

I I I I

IT WAS THAT TIME OF THE YEAR AGAIN. The anniversary of the boy's death again already. It had snuck up on her this time.

Erin couldn't remember what she was supposed to buy for her son. As she thought about the boy they'd prosecuted—he still had dark circles under his eyes when she told the court what had happened behind the curtain—she turned her cart around in the aisle, leaving the sweets behind. She desperately wanted to bake something wholesome for her boy and his class-mates, to take them back to a time before these kinds of things happened to kids, to take them there so she could go back too.

22

THE STORY YOU DON'T TELL OVER DRINKS AT THE BAR NO MATTER HOW DRUNK YOU FIND YOURSELF

THERE WAS A BOY NAMED MILES. He was a few grades older than Poppy, around Chuck's age. He liked to take the younger girls out in his pickup where eventually he'd get them to forget about Catholic morals and give it up. Poppy fell in line when he turned his charm, sparse facial hair and attentions on her one day in the school parking lot while she waited for Chuck to get back from who knows where and give her a lift home. She should have walked. But then she felt special that Miles had picked her instead of Connie who had bigger boobs or Laura who had what old ladies might have called "a reputation," but high school girls just called a spade a spade. Laura was a slut.

Then at seventeen, she saw Bill for the first time, even though she'd known him for years. Bill was great. He was nice. Liked to think he was worldly even though he'd only left town for a few weeks each summer to visit an uncle in Red Deer. He read magazines that talked about world issues, poverty, the AIDS orphan crisis in Africa and Cambodia, struggling endangered species. He always insisted on a call to some sort of never quite defined action, pulling Poppy into his influence. Bill worked for his dad and delivered the Edmonton paper all that year to subscribers who needed a little more than the weekly local, saving money for after graduation.

Adept at painting the kind of pictures that people Poppy's age lived on, Bill made fantasies seem entirely possible, fuelled by sheer enthusiasm. Escape somewhere far away from where they were, some place where they didn't have winters. Bill and Poppy could drink cheap beer and live in a little shack on the beach for an entire season before Poppy would come back to go to community college in the fall. But that daydreaming ended when Bill had the coma and died.

Around that time, Poppy missed her period. Poppy was seventeen and three-quarters. She had her own car now so when it turned out to be something more than stress she booked an appointment at a clinic in Edmonton and spent the three-hour drive searching for reasons why she should tell Bill's parents. If it would help or if it would make things worse than they already were. She settled on letting Bill stay dead.

When Poppy was finally an adult by legal standards, she took a job in the bar at the Holiday Inn and saved for a year. It was a long year with her brother's legal troubles and getting over Bill. She did what she could to keep busy. Tim, Miles and that rig-pig from New Year's Eve. And Miles again. Miles who had gotten married in Poppy's senior year to a nice girl whose dad worked for Poppy's dad, a wedding her parents had been invited to in the church where she was confirmed. Poppy knew she was slipping up all over the place and there was worry in her parents' forced supportive smiles over pot roasts and pork chops. There was talk around town.

When Poppy had saved enough to get out, the men had foreign names, accented English, and couldn't point to where she was from on a map. So she told them she grew up in Toronto. Of course, Poppy was never lonely long, had actually met someone on the plane who was coming from Sweden to study some endangered tortoise that he said could live over a hundred years. Juan-Aarón, who claimed he was *almost* a professional bullfighter, was the fifth in a string of her most recent boyfriends. He kept her busy. He was just fake enough to amuse her, just dreamy enough to have her follow him all over whatever country they were in, just distracting enough so that she could leave her thoughts at home. But even if she could keep thoughts of Bill away, she felt him slip around corners ahead of her, saw him standing against a wall in all the town squares, could make out his shadow in the dark rooms she slept in when her eyes adjusted to the difference.

ALL THOSE TRANS AM DAYS

FIRST DAY IN A NEW SCHOOL. Cory stood in the student parking lot of the Catholic high school. A yellow bus half-full of kids straight from the reserve pulled up to the no-parking zone in front of the building. No, it wasn't all reserve kids. Cory could have been on that bus, sitting near the front next to the window, his knapsack beside him (but he'd move it if someone wanted the seat, like he'd done on the C-Train back in Calgary). The yellow bus picked kids up from the farms too, pulling onto the unpaved shoulder of the highway at the end of dusty private access roads.

"Everyone drives," Cory's dad's girlfriend said from the porch of the new house, a cigarette hanging from her too-red lips. She dropped the still burning butts between the slats of the lumber like a teenager trying to hide her habit from her mother. But the smell lingered on her fingertips and in the fibres of the sweaters she wore with the too-long arms. "Every one," she said, breaking the word into two significantly.

Behind the wheel, Cory had circled the lot three or four times. Each time he came across an open spot, he looked at the vehicles on either side a moment, then pressed the accelerator. Vintage cherry-red Mustang and a shiny new truck. A sport SUV parked lengthwise across three spots so nobody could ding the paint. Trans Am with racing stripes on the hood. An old car with a fin so big it looked like the art his mom used to like. Another Trans Am. A lot full of them.

The beaters parked near the road. Cars with plastic and duct tape where glass should be, ones with rusty floorboards and bungee cords keeping doors and trunks shut. A few vans with no windows at all, the kind that smell like floor cleaner. The owners of the rust-buckets and assorted junkers probably ate lunch in their cars on reject row. Social refuse.

Cory's second-hand car, lovingly spray-painted in the barn one weekend while his dad's girlfriend watched atop stacked hay nearby, was parked three blocks away on an unpaved shoulder near a subdivision under development. First day. First impressions. They used to be about the right jeans, the haircut, maybe a concert T-shirt from a band that was not too popular, but known in the right circles. Something retro. Used to be that was hard enough.

At the dinner table over frozen lasagna, Cory asked his dad's girlfriend, "Did you take the bus?"

Neither of them sat at the head of the table. She pushed the baking tray across the worn wooden surface, offering Cory another scoop of lasagna. It made a grating sound that reminded Cory the tray wasn't real metal.

"Was it terrible?"

"It's how I got to the school. That's all."

In the parking lot next to a car with a metallic blue paint job, the kind that changed colour as the sun caught it, Cory thought, get a job, save for a while, pay his dad back for the insurance first, before too long he could get something that would—

The morning bell rang like a fire alarm. Three times, shrill.

He'd take the bus, until then. There was less shame in having nothing than trying too hard and coming off trashy.

CHECK STOP

BUDDING ACTIVISTS, mostly teenage girls dressed in matching T-shirts, stood next to three RCMP officers in uniforms and hats in the parking lot of the Tourism Saskatchewan office, just off the Yellowhead. It was early evening; the sun was going down quickly and the nerves of the girls picked up as the streetlights buzzed on. Lillian tied a red ribbon to the antenna of a truck and the female driver told Lillian to say hello to her mother. The woman's husband nodded. "Do your homework, you hear now?"

Next. A girl Lillian went to school with. The girl had broken up with her boyfriend of three weeks and was still driving past his house every night. Least that was what Lillian heard. Next. Two red ribbons. One on the antenna next to the gas cap door that wouldn't stay closed. One around the wrist of a toddler in a booster seat that was propped up on an old phone book. The toddler kept kicking the dash with one shoe.

Then a car Lillian recognized from her own driveway arrived. The youngest cop approached her brother with easy, familiar steps. The checkstop was coming to a close. Her box of ribbons donated by MADD was almost gone and these cops weren't getting paid enough to spend the evening away from their TV dinners and after-the-kids-go-to-bed fights with the wife about bills. Lillian had told her brother not to come by, not to drive around this part of town tonight. Told him even though she didn't want to, but he was her brother after all.

27

The cop leaned down and placed his elbows on the window ledge talking to her brother. They laughed, clasped hands. And then the cop turned away and waved at the group of orange-clad girls: it was safe to proceed with the ribbon and the rehearsed chat about the dangers of drinking then getting behind the wheel. Jenna went for it— rumour said she had a thing for Lillian's brother. Lillian intercepted her and walked up to her brother's car.

"What are you doing here?" Lillian began asking sharply, and then as she noticed someone sitting in the passenger seat, she adjusted her tone. The kid from Calgary had very good posture, not like her brother who drove with the seat half reclined. She ran one hand through her curly hair, tugged at a knot.

"Your brother wanted to come and visit," the new kid said. "To say hi."

"Hi," her brother said. "This here is Cory. I was just showing him around. Wanted to drop by and support the cause. Say hi to my friends in uniform."

Lillian shoved a ribbon into her brother's hand. "Get lost." That sounded rude and since Lillian had a reputation for being nice, she added, "It was real nice to meet you Cory."

Lillian's brother dropped the ribbon on the passenger-side weather mat when he reached for the gearshift. If only Lillian had the guts to call the older grisly RCMP officer over to her brother's car and tell him that she knew for a fact that her brother had drugs on his person, that would show her brother that this wasn't a game. Actions had consequences. Rumours exchanged in the hallway said that Lillian's brother was the guy to see if you wanted something. They said he hung around the middle school looking for girls who had matured early. They said he had a pager. Lillian believed everything they said about him, although she hadn't actually seen any of this for herself. She'd only ever seen him smoking it in his car alone, after dinner.

Cory retrieved the ribbon from the mat and wound it around his thumb. "Nice to meet you too. Have fun with this thing."

Then Lillian noticed the older cop calling the other two over to a pickup that had just come down the road. The driver's speech was slurred and there was an open bottle snug between his knees. They had caught one red-handed and now he was going to get what he deserved. Lillian blushed like she had when she won the third grade science fair.

"Poor bastard," Lillian's brother said with a smile.

"It's called justice."

Lillian's brother rolled his eyes and sang in a familiar feathery voice, "That stained glass curtain you're hiding behind..."

Cory picked up where Lillian's brother left off: "Darling, only the good die young." His voice was light, but he sat even straighter in his seat, wrapping and unwrapping the red ribbon from his thumb.

That song about a Catholic schoolgirl virgin, Lillian's brother had been using against her ever since he first heard it, out in the garage with their dad.

BUS STATION DEPARTURES

C RACKED CEMENT NEXT TO A TAXI STAND and Poppy standing there in the sun. She kept one eye on the luggage, her small bag and Juan-Aarón's larger one, as she glanced about the station. She waved to a wispy-haired boy in need of a haircut who sat a dozen metres away on a bench. He was pressing his forehead against the waiting room glass, looking out as she looked in. She was sure she imagined he waved back.

Poppy waited for Juan-Aarón, who had gone inside to buy tickets for the bus heading south along the coastline. He would probably choose to wait out the line of indecisive travellers to buy bottles of water, the plantain chips Poppy liked, stock for the long trip. Poppy didn't particularly want to go south. That was the problem as Poppy saw it; she didn't particularly want to go any place. It was probably time to compose another cheery postcard for her mother, where she wrote a variation on, "Lovely weather here. Oh yes, I am fine. Got a big strong man to look after me so don't worry. Have I mentioned the lovely weather?" But where should she post it from, that was what kept her awake nights.

Poppy turned to look for the boy again. But he had gone as if he hadn't ever been there. She scanned the station. Then she saw him next to a bus. The driver was loading the last of the luggage and began to secure it to the roof with twine. The boy's feet were planted there, his hands on his hips, his ears just a bit too big for his face poking through his hair, the way he looked whenever she had kept him waiting. *Hurry, hurry, Poppy,* it was as if she could hear this phantom. But the lips on the blond boy stayed as they had been, in a flat, disinterested smile.

She knew very well that he was a figment of her imagination, that her therapist guaranteed her he was not real, not there, nowhere but under the ground in his grave, or maybe if Poppy wanted to believe, in heaven waiting. Poppy saw him here because she wanted to see him. In a way. He was trying to tell her something, and if he was then she knew that it was really what she was trying to tell herself that she had to listen to. It was as plain as that. The therapy had been a waste of money.

As the driver descended from the roof and secured the last of the twine, Poppy pulled the colourful scarf from her hair. She felt a little badly for leaving Juan-Aarón like this with no notice because he had been good to her. She tied the scarf to the handle of his luggage. Running now, Poppy was almost desperate to reach the bus before the driver climbed up into his seat and closed the doors on her.

But the driver saw her and waited. "*Billete?*" he asked.

She dug into her pocket and pulled out a handful of bills. She shoved them into his hands. "*Por favor?* Is that enough?"

The driver shrugged, grabbed Poppy's bag, extended his hand indicating that she should board the bus now, and climbed up behind her. He stored her bag in the gap between his seat and the first row of passenger seating.

The bus was quite full, but Poppy managed to find a seat next to a young man. His eyes, they reminded Poppy of Juan-Aarón's and she felt a little sick even though she was sure that right now she felt better than she had in a while. At least she had left him his bag. And the scarf so he'd know she left willingly and wasn't kidnapped or something just as nefarious. That is if his things were still there waiting for him next to the empty taxi stand when he came out of the station with the tickets in his breast pocket, holding four litres of overpriced water, one bottle under each arm, like little missiles.

CUPCAKES AND LITTLE GIRLS

THE MORNING SUN REFLECTED off Christopher's mother's car in lines of light that he could trace all the way back to the sun, until they came to a stop. Christopher climbed out of the car, pulled his backpack off the floor and heaved it onto his shoulder with both bony brown hands. He slammed the door. His mother flinched a little, but all she did was purse her lips tighter. Then he took three big steps and hauled open the rear passenger side door, lifting a tinfoil-covered tray from the seat. He held the tray in one hand as he slammed the rear door too, for emphasis. Christopher didn't bother to wave goodbye to his mother. Outside of the car, Christopher couldn't see the lines of light coming from the sun anymore.

Up the steps and into the school and down the hall into his classroom with a quick shuffle. He was late. Mom's damn fault, he thought, using the word church told him was bad. It was his birthday; God would probably have to forgive him at least today. Tomorrow he would repent.

"Is this your special treat, Christopher?" his teacher, Ms. Wright, asked. She was a tall blonde woman who was just out of school as she kept telling her class, trying to relate. Christopher thought she was old. Maybe older than his mom.

Instead of answering Ms. Wright, he handed the tinfoil tray over and shrugged out of his jacket. Then he took his seat. Christopher pulled out his workbook and moved his face close to the page, attempting to concentrate on multiplication. When he could no longer think about the math problem without obsessing over the approaching birthday celebration, he dared himself to look at the table at the back of the room.

It was a girl's birthday too. Her name was Alyssa. She had curly hair and was a little spoiled by Ms. Wright who didn't make Alyssa work when she cried about it. Next to his mom's tray, a plastic dollar-store tray from last Christmas, stood a fancy cupcake holder. And in the cupcake holder were pink frosting-covered cakes. Each one of them supported an unlit pastel candle. Christopher turned back to his workbook, not eager for recess when Ms. Wright would get the class to sing for Alyssa and Christopher, forcing the extra syllables into the lines of the song. Then she would uncover the birthday snacks and invite the students to each pick one. She was trying to teach them something, but Christopher didn't know what.

The kids weren't mean. They just didn't try out Christopher's mom's baking, gravitating like kids do to fluffy, iced sweets. While he wanted a cupcake pretty badly, Christopher moved toward the table at the back of the room and reached for a slice of the zucchini-carrot cake his mom had spent yesterday evening in the kitchen making for him. If he didn't eat his mom's cake, they'd all think that she must not like her son very much if for his birthday she baked something that he didn't even like. This bite of cake in his mouth was proof that he was loved.

So Christopher helped himself to a second piece when Ms. Wright wasn't looking. There was plenty left. Between bites he craned his to make sure that his classmates were watching him.

THE SATURDAY AFTERNOON FIRE

P ATRONS OF THE HOTEL had to turn off the Yellowhead and take the business access road well before they passed the hotel itself. A wide bank of grass running parallel to the highway divided the two roads. If a driver intended on getting to the hotel—maybe it was a high school student wanting to sneak in the service door for a complimentary swim in the pool, or maybe it was a rig-pig wanting to buy his lunch from the grease-trap grill next door to the hotel, or someone who needed to wash his truck at the 24-hour car wash on the adjacent lot—he would have to catch the access road or he'd drive several blocks past his destination before he had the chance to turn around. There was no direct access.

On this particular afternoon, the bank of grass was covered with bystanders stomping down the new growth. Pickup trucks had stopped in the far right lane of the highway. Some of them had their blinkers on, but most of the drivers pulling over to watch the fire figured the cops would have their hands too full to bother passing out tickets to spectators.

Black smoke rose from the six-story building, billowing out of broken windows. Sergeant W. Leroy stood next to his patrol car, watching the fire. "Everyone got out safe," Leroy said when a reporter from the *Border Dispatch* walked up to him with a notebook in hand. "I'm only here to make sure all bystanders stay back out of the way of the professionals."

"Any idea how it started, Sergeant?"

Leroy shrugged. "It might have been someone who fell asleep with a cigarette lit."

"Your source?"

"I figure. Smoking, it's not just the cancer, you know?"

The reporter smiled indulgently, then excusing himself, ambled off toward a firefighter who was standing next to the fire engine. The reporter needed another angle on the story of the year if he was going to sell his share of advertising space this week. This story, it might free him up from a few weeks of advertising sales duty. It might get him a raise, or get picked up by national news.

"I hear it was for insurance purposes," a man with a Husky trucker hat said to the tiny brunette standing next to him. She nodded without giving him the benefit of eye contact. There was a fire in progress after all.

Out on the road, in the right-hand lane, Cory stood in the bed of his dad's girlfriend's truck next to a dozen bags of groceries to get a better look. His dad had left the keys in the ignition and wandered off towards the fire, holding his girlfriend's hand. The two of them had left Cory with the groceries and the truck so they could get up close and watch a hotel burn down. Cory climbed up on top of the cab, gaining a few more feet.

"Hey," Lillian said tentatively from the tailgate. "I'm parked way down the road. Guess what I just heard?"

"You want to come up here?" Cory asked. "Better view."

"I have to find my brother," she said.

Cory cocked his head in the direction of the burning building. "He wasn't working today, was he?"

Lillian rolled her eyes way up into her hairline and Cory didn't know if that meant yes or no.

"He told me that Steve—Do you know Steve? Dark hair, used to date Sandy, Derek's sister. Apparently, he started the fire." Lillian watched Cory's reaction. "It wasn't on purpose. Apparently."

"Oh."

"He tried to set firecrackers off and some leftover roofing material from the renos last year caught fire. Weird, eh?" She waved and moved on. "I really have to find my brother," she said.

The town gossiped for days: cigarettes, a firecracker accident, arson, a romantic tryst gone wrong, insurance scams, everything else and the kitchen sink too.

When the paper came out four days later, nobody had seemed to have gotten it right. An inexperienced high school student working weekends at the hotel in room service was sent down to the laundry since the laundry girl had called in sick. In the interview, she revealed that she wasn't really sick, but her three-year-old was and couldn't go to daycare on account of his fever. The high school boy stuffed the coveralls from room 306 into the industrial machine, wiping the oil from his hands on his jeans. He took the stairs back up to the kitchen to wait for the load to finish so he could transfer it to the dryer like his sister had told him to do when he called begging for a girl's insight into these kinds of things. The rig worker's laundry combusted in the machine and the resulting fireball engulfed the linens stored in the basement. The fire spread quickly. There were no injuries. That was what the fire chief said in his report.

The student was asking his employers to buy him a new pair of jeans. He bragged around the hallways in school that if they didn't cover his jeans, he would sue.

AFTER DINNER CONVERSATIONS

T HE TABLE WAS SET FOR THREE, but an additional place-mat was set out across from Mike's usual spot. The veneer on the Lansing's formal dining table was scratched by years of the kids doing their homework without first putting a magazine or something hard down under sheets of loose-leaf paper. Mike could trace the sixes and nines in the formal dining table, a gift from his in-laws. For a while now, the table had been pushed against the railing dividing the kitchen from the sunken living room, but the empty placemat stayed at its place there against the railing. Barb said it was for visual balance, but Mike knew better.

Frank's cellphone vibrated, skating along the table. He glanced at the screen for a second before standing up, and gathering his plate in one hand. Tucking two fingers against his wine glass, he counterbalanced them with his thumb like a vice. "You'll have to excuse me," he said as he placed the dishes in the sink and made a cursory attempt at rinsing them. "There's been an accident on the Yellowhead. They need a few of us out there to clear the cars away."

"No problem." Mike stretched his arms above his head, feel-ing his spine cracking.

"Will we see you tomorrow?" Barb asked. She ran a finger around the rim of her empty glass. "I'm making meatloaf. There'll be plenty extra."

"Thanks," Frank said. He gathered his coat from the banister. Barb made as if to stand up, so Frank said, "No need to see me out." Then he was gone.

Mike kept busy fiddling with things on the table, moving the pepper mill back onto the lazy Susan, folding his napkin into a perfect square, refilling his wine glass. Finally he offered the bottle to his wife.

"I don't feel like it. Why don't you finish it?"

"Babe, I've been thinking. We should…buy a smaller place. Downsize. Rent something on the Saskatchewan side, closer to work."

"That is not happening." Barb grabbed the wine bottle and filled her glass for the first time that evening. "You can tell Frank dinner will be ready at six sharp tomorrow. I'm expecting him. Six sharp. Both of you."

"Can't we eat just the two of us every once in a while? If it's not Frank, it's Patricia staying for the weekend. And if it's not Patty-cake, it's one of your old co-workers from the beauty counter."

"And before that," she said without malice, "it was our kids."

Mike rose to clear the table for his wife. He cleared everything but her glass, and rinsed the dishes in the sink with the scrubber wand like she liked him to do before he placed them in the dishwasher, cups on the top rack, the plates on the bottom and the cutlery in the little caddy hooked to the side. "I have a week's holiday coming up. We should go somewhere. Get away."

"We could go to Edmonton, stay with—"

"No, I mean, let's leave for a while. Take a vacation from Chuck and Poppy and Patricia and Frank."

"You can't take a vacation from life Michael. Haven't you figured it out yet?"

"We can. People do it all the time! What do you think your daughter is doing?"

"Oh? She's *my* daughter now?"

"You know what I mean," he said. Mike left the dishwasher ajar and walked out of the kitchen in search of the foam stress ball one of the secretaries had given him in the Secret Santa pool last year. From the master bedroom on the main floor, he called, "I'm getting out of here. For a week. Somewhere warm where they don't have problems you can't cure with rum punch. Am I booking double occupancy?"

"Don't forget to tell Frank I'll be expecting him at six."

In the morning, Mike Lansing reported to work without filing the vacation request form with personnel management. Frank came to dinner Wednesday and Thursday that week.

JUST LIKE IT SHOULD

B ARBARA'S PARENTS WEREN'T FRUSTRATED, irritated or angry when she told them over roast chicken that she wasn't going to go on to study Sociology at university in the fall, that she would rather stay in town and work at the beauty counter at Sears giving old women free makeovers on weekday afternoons, then watching TV in the living room most evenings with big-armed and warm-hearted Mike. Her mother didn't even furrow her manicured eyebrows like she normally would have, while her husband cleared his throat to begin the lecture that would steer their oldest daughter in the right direction. Barbara's father asked her to pass the bowl of mashed potatoes down the table even though the bowl was within easy reach of his arm. Her mother said, "That sounds like a plan, honey. We'd be happy to have you around the house for a little while longer." Her eyebrows were expressionless. Patricia started talking about the dance next week at school.

What Barbara did not know was that Mike had met with her father sometime the week before in that old ceremony between father and potential son-in-law where Mike got down to the business of asking for permission to ask for Barbara's hand. Her parents promptly stopped worrying about topping up the college fund and how Barbara would fare in the big city's downtown campus. Thirteen days later, Barbara got a new car—not the sporty sedan she wanted to buy for herself but a four-door, wood-paneled station wagon—a Bob Marley cassette tape and a modest diamond ring for her birthday.

Their engagement lasted a little less than a year. Barbara's parents spent her college fund on a white wedding with all the frills in their backyard one idyllic afternoon in July, the peak of the short summer. Patricia played the role of bridesmaid for the high school sweethearts. That very week they took the step of securing a mortgage from the town credit union with Barbara's parents as co-signers. At nineteen, Barbara was fully grown-up with a house of her own, a little yard where the new puppy played and a husband who recently received a promotion at his job. He brought home a bottle of expensive wine to celebrate and they laughed and watched TV.

When schoolyard friends moved away to go into the city to follow their dreams or boyfriends, Barbara found herself in the company of the girls who had dropped out of school to have babies. Barbara would spend her free afternoons sitting on park benches watching toddlers play in sandboxes, stealing a bite or two of an afternoon snack as she chatted with young mothers who smoked cigarettes while they calmed their toddlers' younger siblings, sometimes passing the babies off to Barbara while they chased their ambulatory children away from the road. Soon enough Barbara joined the young mothers with her own baby and she watched him grow from that bench.

While Barbara held her daughter and watched her toddler son running around the park with the other kids in his new trainers, she thought about her upcoming twenty-second birthday. Mike had organized a sitter for the kids, a co-worker's teenage daughter. Mike told his wife that he wanted to take her to one of the nice restaurants off the highway so they could celebrate "being on track."

Life was just like it should be.

DUMPED

JUAN-AARÓN SURVEYED THE STATION as if he were taking it all in, and like travellers who were obsessively early for departures, he had nothing consuming to attend to except being ready for his bus to pull out of the terminal at some predetermined, scheduled time. He strolled across the staging area where the diesel-fuelled buses waited for passengers to unload before a man with a basket of cleaning supplies and one leg slightly shorter than the other climbed aboard to tend to the bathroom.

Juan-Aarón took a seat next to a uniformed bus driver, a small grey-haired man wrinkled by long hours, on one of the few benches in the outdoor section of the terminal. Three coaches were loading passengers, their noisy diesel engines shaking the people aboard as they tried to claim seats. Juan-Aarón's right leg moved in tempo with the engines. The two men exchanged ritual pleasantries and Juan-Aarón listened patiently before asking if the driver had noticed a foreign woman with blunt short brown hair waiting by the taxi stand. "She was wearing a yellow sundress, has a figure like a proper movie star," he said, illustrating his words with generous hand gestures. Juan-Aarón waved casually in the direction of his luggage, where the multi-coloured scarf hung limp in the humid air.

The driver hunched down into the bench before answering Juan-Aarón's question with a raspy inquiry, "Did you lose her?"

Juan-Aarón shrugged and smiled bringing his scar into view. "Misplaced her. For now."

"I saw." The driver pulled himself up straighter on the bench, to reach into his shirt pocket, so he could offer Juan-Aarón a hand-rolled cigarette from a silver compact, engraved on the top with initials. "She boarded a bus for the north. Hire a taxi, you can be waiting when she disembarks. For more *pisto* certainly. She's worth it."

Juan-Aarón took the cigarette and matches the driver offered him in friendship even though as a rule Juan-Aarón did not smoke. "I am unworried," he said, patting his breast pocket. "Even foreign women shaped like movie stars need their passport to cross the international borders."

As exhaust from a departing bus enveloped the bench, the men shared a deep, smoky belly laugh.

DRIVING LESSONS

O N A TEMPERATE SPRING-LIKE DAY in February, in a neighbourhood of cookie-cutter houses iced in pale blues, greens and yellows where the streets are wide and empty, a man taught his daughter how to drive. The red car lurched forward, then stalled. It was Sunday.

"It would help," Lillian said, "if you'd quit laughing at me. Someone once told me that driving is all about confidence."

"Lily, I say it's about releasing the clutch slowly. If you don't, you'll stall out in an intersection and get yourself T-boned like Dirk Ingleson did that once," he said as he cleared his throat violently. When the phlegm tasted like blood, Lillian's dad had started swallowing the crap, rather than subjecting his family to the sight of it.

Dirk Ingleson was legendary in Lillian's house. He was her dad's instructive example. Don't forget to wear wrist guards, he said. Dirk Ingleson broke both his arms on roller skates. The doctor told his mother that if he'd been wearing the appropriate safety equipment that would not have happened. Don't smoke!, he said. Dirk Ingleson suffered from emphysema, all those cigarettes he polished off growing up. Do you want to contract emphysema, kids? I didn't think so. He said, Dirk Ingleson didn't listen to his father's good sense and he ended up "landscaping that judge's lawn all summer. Free of com-pen-sa-tion!" Lillian could finish most of the cautionary tales mimicking her dad's voice, she had heard them so often. Her father had one for everything: why you should always shop with a

47

grocery list; rules about visiting graveyards; how to siphon gasoline from a nearby tank when yours has run dry and it's too late to call a friend and too early to fill up at the pump (be sure to leave a twenty and plenty of goodwill under the wiper blade). Lillian wondered if there was ever a Dirk Ingleson, but her dad's words were a gospel not to be questioned.

Lillian turned the ignition key, but not without first checking to be sure she was in neutral. That was a lesson she had already learned. Clutch, first gear, just a little gas, the car started to move, lurched. Stalled. She gripped the steering wheel firmly, the tips of her nails coated in chipped black paint, her fingers now beginning to pale. Her father had one hand braced against the dashboard; he placed the other on his daughter's knee, laughing under his breath. At least he wasn't coughing.

A car pulled up alongside them before Lillian could think about going at it again. It was the RCMP, the lights of the sedan flashing but the siren quiet as if this wasn't official enough for the full show. The cop left his hat on the passenger seat and walked over to Lillian's side of the car. He rapped twice on the window. After a nod from her dad, Lillian turned the crank.

"Licence and registration," the cop said on script. "Yours too, sir."

Lillian lifted her hips off the seat so she could reach into the back pocket of her jeans. Trying as hard as she could to keep her hand from shaking, she passed her learner's permit to the cop but dropped it before his hand opened to receive it. The permit fell to the ground in the sand and the debris revealed by melting snow, a diet pop can crushed flat and pieces of paper in assorted stages of decomposition.

The cop picked her permit up, took Lillian's father's licence from him by reaching across Lillian to get it, then retreated to his vehicle where the lights were still flashing. Lillian and her father waited in silence. They both looked straight ahead, Lillian thinking *clutch, gear, gas, clutch*, sneaking glances in the rear-view mirror at the cop. When the cop came back, he gave them their licences and a ticket for driving dangerously, endangering the public. "This is a family neighbourhood, after all." All the emphasis was on family. It was as if Lillian's brother were in the car with them, as if his reputation followed them from their neighbourhood where residents had old couches on their porches that were rotting and almost always damp to the nicer part of town where couches left at the end of these clipped yards on garbage day would find their way into someone's living room, displacing some other scavenged couch to the porch and the old porch couch to the end of the road. Recycling, upcycling.

After Lillian and her dad swapped seats, he spoke first. "We should call it quits. I'll talk to my boss, trade her in for an automatic." He cleared his throat again, rivalling the sound of the engine as it whined in low gear. "There was a nice Nissan on the lot."

Lillian's father seemed too big for the little car as he shook it with his cough. Lillian ran her hand over the dash, admiring the little nicks in the plastic that she felt but couldn't see unless the light was just right. It didn't smell like an old car, more like the deodorizing spray her mother used on the cat box. But underneath that, she thought she could smell cloves. The car had a history Lillian could only imagine. And for a few days the car and the possibilities had belonged to her.

But her father was right. The driving lessons had to stop. Her father brought home the Nissan's bulky keys on Monday, lay on the sofa for three weeks, only pulling himself out from under the scratchy wool blanket to urinate. One day he took Lillian's brother for a man-to-man chat in the stick-shift sports car bought for his sixteenth birthday and Lillian's dad died the next day.

Lillian's brother told her to go to court, to fight the ticket. Lillian drove to city hall in the boxy automatic and paid. It was the right thing to do.

SCHOOL PHOTOS

CHRISTOPHER SAT AT THE KITCHEN TABLE with his homework spread out in front of him as he argued with his mother. On the far edge of the table, a piece of neon paper reminded students to tell their parents about the upcoming picture day. "I should have thrown it in the trash," Christopher said, scraping the bevelled edge of the table with his pencil to chip off the varnish. "Then we wouldn't be in a fight."

Erin stood over the stove still wearing her blue scrubs, and stirred a pot of rice even though Erin's mother had told her never to lift the lid when cooking rice. Patience made perfect rice. "We are not fighting." Blue was a good colour for Erin. It highlighted her eyes.

"I really don't want pictures."

"Why not?"

"I just really don't."

She moved over to the table, cleared Christopher's homework off to one side and placed the note from school on top of the pile. "Milk? Or do you want a can of cola?"

"Milk is fine," Christopher said. He was not giving in that easily.

Erin finished setting the table. Poured two glasses of skim milk. Put finishing touches on their meal. She did not clang the pots or close the cupboards a little too firmly.

Christopher figured that on account of his mother's unusual silence, he'd won. He wouldn't have to wear a sweater vest and wait in line with the other kids and walk up to sit under the lights and have some man fiddle with Christopher's nappy hair so that it would sit right. He wouldn't have to wait to see how the pictures turned out and have the talk with his mother about which of the three poses he liked best. Wouldn't have to watch her pick the one he didn't like even after she asked him.

"What happens," Erin said after she had chewed a mouthful of rice and stir-fried vegetables, "when some creep abducts you through your bedroom window one night and after a few weeks of living like some caged animal, the creep decides that it's time to axe-murder you? What am I supposed to do then?"

Christopher swallowed his food and took a good look at his mom. He almost expected her eyes to bug out of her face like the parent's eyes always did on those Family Channel shows. But Erin just looked like what his mom normally looked like, except her eyes were sad like Christopher was used to seeing when she had a bad shift at work.

"What picture am I going to give them to print in the newspaper, Christopher?"

Christopher looked away from his mom and studied the damage he'd done to her kitchen table, uncovering the light coloured wood from beneath the varnish.

"I'll look like an incompetent mother."

Christopher said, "I'll get the pictures done." He took a forkful of his meal and started to chew mechanically. "Even though nobody is gonna axe-murder me, mom," he added.

"Will you wear the green sweater?"

"Fine."

"How do you like the rice?"

"It's good, mom."

In response, Erin got up from the table, walked over to the stove and carried the pot of rice over to her son's still full plate. She served him more rice.

ALL THOSE WEEPING WILLOWS

A WEEPING WILLOW GREW IN THE BACKYARD of Chuck's childhood home. It was old when they moved in, had probably been there since before the company who built the houses broke the land, hollowed out the dirt to set the foundations. When they were building around here, the tall willows sprinkled around the grounds were a nice addition that would help the newly constructed neighbourhood look like it was established. The trees gave picture-perfect houses credibility.

Chuck chased his sister around that tree when he was rambunctious and high on caffeine from too many bottles of pop. He tackled his sister and whipped her with the limber vines when he wanted to hurt her, revenge for some slight or another, or sometimes just because. And he gave her a boost into the air so that she could swing on a handful of the strong, drooping branches when he felt bad for leaving her behind after the neighbourhood boys came calling with their bicycles, strips of cardboard clipped to the spokes. The boys would ride up and down the street, wheeling through the runoff from broken water mains, the cardboard clip-clip-clipping in the weekend air.

Around the time Chuck started high school, the city contractors let themselves into the yards on Chuck's block and spray-painted orange crosses on the trees that were to be removed. By the time the snow started to fall, the weeping willows were gone. They were destroying important neighbourhood infra-structure, that was the official reason, noted on the flyer left taped to the screen door the day before the crews brought their machines into Chuck's yard. The trees never intended to squeeze the pipes buried underground, crippling the aquamarine industrial plastic. The trees never intended to dislodge the fence posts that separated backyards from the alleyway. They were just stretching, growing.

Chuck sat in his room, perched in the window seat his mother had gone to such trouble to upholster with a John Deere tractor print, watching the city workers systematically take the tree apart. Starting from the top, they erased it as if it had never belonged in the yard where Chuck grew up. After that Chuck yelled at his mom about fixing the same crap for dinner night after night, even though Tuesday's hamburger casserole was usually one of his favourites. Things changed after the willows disappeared from the neighbourhood, though nobody else seemed to notice. Not even Poppy. She took off with her girlfriends and rode her bike—a hand-me-down from Chuck after his growth spurt—through rain puddles while Chuck sat in his room with the door locked.

Now Chuck sat on a bench bolted into the cement in the prison yard, trying to make out what kind of trees lay beyond the fencing and the wire. They swayed in the wind like the willows he remembered, but Chuck did not trust his eyes. Lately, he saw what he wanted to see. He decided this was a coping mechanism, a way to pass through the days that he had left in here without feeling them. Maybe Chuck had always seen what he wanted to see, didn't see what was right in front of him until it had smacked him in the face.

"What are you looking at?" another prisoner said, sitting down.

Chuck cocked his head in the direction of the willows. "In the distance. The trees."

The prisoner fiddled with a worn Rubik's Cube. "I see the fence, the parking lot. I don't see no forest."

Even though years had passed since the tree had been hauled away as firewood, its skinny branches thrown into a chipper, and Chuck supposed he should devote his energy to other things, he still felt quiet anger for what had happened to the trees.

THE YELLOWHEAD

HALFWAY BETWEEN EDMONTON AND SASKATOON, bisected by the highway, there was a city. John learned how to drive on the highway, but the instructor always told him to turn around just as they picked up speed. John crashed once on that highway, on his way to Edmonton for a weekend of youthful debauchery on Whyte Avenue, totalled his adoptive mother's car. He promised her he would never do it again. He reminded her how lucky he was that she had picked him out of all God's children when she could have had a white baby instead. The sentiment was something she herself said, something that always seemed to calm her like a balm. On the highway, John had been pulled over by the cops, given tickets, warnings, a black eye once.

"Get out," his mother said, three months before his high school graduation ceremony, an inflated choreographed parade for parents who didn't expect to see another graduation. His mother did not come to watch him collect his diploma. John did not have pictures of himself wearing that funny hat, surrounded by family.

After graduation, John spent a year in Saskatoon, a year down the highway. When he came back, there was a keloid scar across one cheek, beginning just below the left eye. He took a job at the Husky station on the highway, started dating a girl called Erin he used to know but hadn't slept with in high school, picked up a nasty habit of smoking while he worked the pumps.

In bed, John told Erin about a job he'd been thinking of taking.

"Get outta here?" she said. "I don't think so, Johnny. I never liked the big city."

John's estranged mother died in the hospital on the Saskatchewan side, three days after Erin asked him to clean the junk out of the hall closet. The morning after his mother passed on to her home in heaven, John packed four black garbage bags in the trunk of his mother's car, went for a seven dollar wax & wash, stopped at the Tim Hortons to kiss Erin through the drive-through window. He knew her nursing textbook was open on the counter beside the sink. It always was.

"You shaved."

"How do I look?"

"The dead don't care what you look like," she said, leaning out the window for another kiss, a peck on the forehead this time. She had to lean so far out the window, she almost fell, caught off balance by her big belly. So she started pulling herself back inside the drive-through window before she made a real scene. Or hurt herself. Or the baby.

"I'm sorry." John grabbed her hand as she pulled away. "I-I know you...you liked it."

He took a left out onto the highway heading west when the convoy of transport trucks cutting through town on their way across the country cleared for a minute. The window was rolled down, the wind warm and, as John picked up speed along the road, the country radio station began to cut out. At first static interrupted half a word. As he moved away from the signal tower the cuts became more pronounced, until when he turned into the left hand lane to overtake a transport truck, the signal cut out forever.

The trucking company dispatched a crisis worker to the scene.

OUT OF TOWN

TWENTY KILOMETRES OUT OF TOWN was a long way, even
if it only took a few songs' coasting time on the radio to
hit the city limit sign. Cory had to wake up a good half
hour earlier than his friends to manage to get to school on
time, earlier still if it was winter and there had been a storm
the night before. When his friends called it a night, Cory
had to stay awake long enough to drive home, was starting to
get used to the sound of the rumble strips on the edge of the
Yellowhead when he dozed off. Except when he slept on the
couch at Lillian's brother's house.

Mrs. Sheedy was becoming accustomed to seeing Cory in her
house. She caught him in the hallway as he was coming out of
her bathroom and before Cory could make his way back down
the stairs to her kids and her television, asked him if everything
was alright at home. "I mean, no one's... They aren't...?"

"No. No, really, I swear. Things are good."

When Mrs. Sheedy reached out as if to touch Cory's arm,
Cory insisted that nothing was wrong. "I just live out of town.
It's far to drive."

"Okay, but if you need anything," she said. "You ask is all
you do."

Mrs. Sheedy waited until the kids left for school and she
cleaned the cereal bowls with the leftover chocolate milk coat-
ing the bottoms, before she called the CAS.

"We'll look into the situation, ma'am. The stepmother is
known to us."

Mrs. Sheedy cleared her throat into the phone. "They aren't married. Just living together while the kid sleeps in *my* basement most nights and eats *my* groceries."

After work on Thursday, Cory paid for gasoline with a handful of gas bar coupons from the newly built Superstore and a twenty he had saved from last week's pay cheque. When he pulled up the drive of his dad's girlfriend's family home, the living room curtains parted, fluttered.

While he was dumping his laundry into the machine right out of his school bag, Cory's dad's girlfriend stood in the doorway of the laundry room. "You haven't been home in a while."

"I'm busy at school."

"Your dad hasn't seen you in a while," she said and left Cory to his laundry.

On Monday, the guidance counsellor called Cory in to see him. His office was long and narrow and windowless. Cory remembered the office from his first week, when the guidance counsellor welcomed him to school and disclosed in a monotone which credits the district had decided to accept for transfer. An unfamiliar woman wearing thin wire glasses sat in one of the two school-issue plastic chairs.

"Hi Cory," the guidance counsellor said. "We just wanted to talk to you."

"Hello Cory," the woman said. "It's come to our attention that you're having some problems at home."

"We just want to talk," the guidance counsellor interjected.

"It's important, Cory, that you know there are programs out there to help young Natives adjust—"

"Cory isn't..." The guidance counselor let the unfinished sentence linger.

She tucked her name badge into her breast pocket. "If you're being abused... It's important that you tell us, Cory. So we can help you deal with your situation."

Cory let his backpack slip off his shoulder and fall to the ground. It didn't make any loud noises, padded by his newly cleaned laundry. Suddenly, he felt guilty.

"Why don't you tell us why you keep spending the night at the Sheedy house?" the guidance counsellor asked.

"Cory, we're here to discuss any issues you might be having."

"I," Cory began sheepishly, "live out of town."

"We cannot have a meaningful discussion if you do not talk to us honestly, Cory." The woman readjusted her glasses.

"It's a long drive," Cory said.

"Is that all you have to say?" the guidance counsellor asked. Then he checked his watch with a downward flick of his eyes, as if to provide plausible deniability if Cory wanted to complain that the guidance counsellor cared more about the lunch bell ringing in fifteen minutes than about Cory's deep teenage angst.

"We're going to have to schedule weekly sessions until we can resolve this," the woman said, addressing the guidance counsellor.

Dismissed, Cory gathered his bag and decided to head out to lunch early. That night he drove Lillian's brother home, saying that he had to get back tonight or his dad would have a fit. Then Cory drove towards the edge of town and pulled into the Canadian Tire parking lot, looking for a suitable place to park his car overnight.

LETTERS FOR CONVICTS

ALL KINDS OF MAIL ENTERED THE PRISON, letters from family and friends, from lovers and wives (sometimes one from each on the very same day), bad-news letters from lawyers, from collection agencies, and notes from concerned citizens, church groups. But the mail most often found on the prison cart was assorted magazines, correspondence from Publishers Clearing House and letters from pen pals. Sometimes the odd flyer advertising a two-for-one special on pizza would slip through, somehow. An inmate could salivate over it for a few minutes, could remember the best pizza he ever had and how it had burnt the roof of his mouth and how the pain was worth it as he finished the pie surrounded by his friends. Surrounded by beer. By a woman who loved him. Or a woman who didn't but didn't care.

Chuck only allowed himself a subscription to one periodical. He read the *Edmonton Journal*, but often got issues a few days later than people on the outside, the news only a little stale. Most of the other inmates had subscriptions to men's magazines like *Maxim* or *Hunting and Fishing Quarterly* and, of course, those skin magazines that kept the men in fantasies in a place without trees or natural light or beaches littered with bikinied blondes. Chuck focused on the news that dealt with crime, with criminals, wallowing in his guilt, in that pain. Sometimes if he felt like he deserved a break from reading the paper or if his eyes had started to go buggy from the fluorescent lights on the newsprint, he would attempt the crossword puzzle. More often than not, Chuck could solve Monday's.

When Chuck first arrived, he threw out those letters with bold statements like "You may already be a winner!" and "Mr. So and So, your name has *already* been entered in our grand prize draw," without slipping his finger under the envelope flaps. But he watched other prisoners attach the shiny stamps to the winner's label and order gadgets they would never use for one more entry into the draw. Chuck's cellmate was religious when it came to Publishers Clearing House, if nothing else.

"You could be throwing a million dollars in the trash."

"Did your ex-wife like that micro-fibre hair-wrap towel thing?"

His cellmate nodded. "She said it was a pretty damn good birthday present. Even if the wrap was a little too tight on her head. And it got my name in the grand prize draw twice. Two chances more than you, sucker. I'm gonna provide for my family."

When the other prisoners weren't busy dreaming of the money they might have already won, they were writing letters to strangers who had signed up to correspond with men in provincial and federal institutions. The letters started off awkwardly, my name is blank and here are the things you need to know about me, like on a first date. What should I know about you (but it's okay if you dance around the reason why you're locked up—at least at first—because this is your pain and I'm not ready for you to know I want it to be my pain too)? Sometimes these correspondences matured into relationships on visitor's day, when after a suitable amount of time, a prisoner charmed his way into someone's life. It was usually a woman, usually overweight or recently divorced from her used-to-be boy-next-door and now rotten-bastard-of-a-man who was the father to her school-aged children. Sometimes, if the inmate was released, they would get married or at least live together for a while sharing everything. At least that was the story the websites promising to hook inmates up with long-distance friends liked to suggest with testimonials by women with names like Tammy, Sheila and L'Atisha.

Chuck didn't get letters from his parents, aunts, uncles or grandparents. But that was by request. He was sure his mother would have sent weekly correspondence in longhand where she recounted the happenings at home and in town, what they had for dinner, whose kid brother was delivering the paper this month. She would have reminded him that it wasn't his fault, not really. That Christ would forgive him if no one else could. That small towns didn't easily forget. But Chuck accepted the postcards that Poppy would send occasionally. They were bright, commercial advertisements for whatever city she had found herself in. And the only thing she wrote was "Love from your sister." Getting her postcards made him shiver inside, but Chuck didn't have the heart to tell her to stop.

When the mail was distributed Monday afternoon, Chuck sat on his bed with last Friday's edition of the news and a letter from Publishers Clearing House. He tore open the letter and for the first time began to read it and let himself remember the last good pizza he'd had and the last good pain he'd felt.

DEATH THROUGH THE FLOORBOARDS

POPPY RENTED A SMALL ROOM on the top floor of a tourist shop on the main street in the seaside town. The stall sold different handmade Mayan crafts, colourful scarves and tiny rag dolls, the kind of souvenir to bring back for an aunt, a kid cousin or a long-suffering cat. The family made the items outside sitting on milk crates in front of their stall, an elderly woman nestled between the children, the children shooing away a stray dog with floppy ears, bringing what Poppy thought was a kind of immediacy to the otherwise identical souvenirs on the block. This was real. The family of six lived on the second floor. Poppy could hear them talking in Spanish over the sound of the elderly woman's coughing.

The third floor flat used to be rented to a painter, or so Poppy figured. A vase of dead flowers placed dead centre was surrounded by a layer of dust on the dining table. The flowers and the shadow they cast onto the far wall looked painterly. Poppy could admit to herself that was why she had decided to rent this particular set of rooms instead of something on the coast like what she and Bill had talked about when they were lovesick kids.

As the sun fell low in the sky and the shadow of the flowers was at its largest, Poppy sat in the main room, the sounds from the open window wafting over her: a dog whining under her window, someone throwing a bucket of water on the road. At first Poppy listened to the tourists whose voices were louder, carried further, than the voices of locals. But those voices always deteriorated into fighting, angry and bitter and cold. To forget, she keyed herself into the locals, translating what Spanish she remembered from the *Learn Spanish in Only Ten Minutes a Day* book she had checked out of the library and subsequently slipped into her suitcase when she left home months ago. Was her mother still getting calls for the overdue fines? Poppy had left the book behind long ago. The room became very dark and then she could only hear the old woman's coughing and sharp breathing.

Poppy figured the woman was lying down in the room directly under her room since when the woman coughed, it was as if Poppy were in the room with her. The sound of the woman dying, the flowers on the table and the lingering presence of a boy that Poppy used to know rested in the room with her. It was past the family's usual dinner time and a silence settled there, settled in with Poppy. Everyone in the house was listening to the sounds of the old woman as she struggled to keep up with her body's need for oxygen.

Never one to be affected by the goings-on around her, Poppy was now having trouble breathing steadily as she listened to this family's private business. It wasn't enough that she knew wherever she went she would see the only person she had really known who had died, now she was listening to someone dying through the floorboards. Even though this woman was old, still, this was too close to death, too familiar. And today when she rifled through her bags searching for her passport so she could catch a bus and head for the border in the morning, she noticed that it wasn't where she had left it. It was gone. Poppy would not be leaving in the morning.

She thought she heard a sharp "shh" as the woman resumed coughing, a little less loudly. It was probably directed at the children, but Poppy took off her shoes just in case she had been intruding on their deathwatch. She couldn't tune the woman out. The coughing turned into wheezing, and as Poppy got lost in her thoughts, she worried the wheezing had faded. On her hands and knees now, Poppy pressed her ear to the floor, then lay down on the floor from which she had yet to sweep the sand from the road, so she could hear even the smallest of sounds.

THE ONLY BLACK KID

I N ELEMENTARY SCHOOL, most kids thought he was adopted. Insofar as they imagined Christopher's home life, it was a lot like theirs, except that they had sisters and brothers and Christopher didn't actually belong to his parents like they did to theirs. The stork had gotten lost, but Christopher's mom decided to keep him anyway. Christopher was a good example of charity to less fortunate human beings like they learned in Sunday school. At Christmas and birthdays, the children's parents would try to encourage them to donate a few dollars of their monetary gifts to those less fortunate ones. Usually this meant dropping money in a box at the checkout counter at Safeway or putting some extra change in the church plate when it made the rounds.

"Christopher's parents are so generous to the poor, they brought him all the way from Africa!" one of the little know-it-alls in his second grade class declared as the teacher was leading discussion on Christian values one afternoon.

Automatically, the teacher said, "That's great, Crystal." It was inappropriate to talk to seven-year-olds about interracial couples and with what had happened to Christopher's father, the teacher figured that glossing over the problem would be best. For everyone. And this had opened the door to discuss geography.

In middle school, Christopher told kids he was adopted. Nobody questioned him. But he never really knew what to say when kids asked him what his dad did for a living. Did he work in the corporate Husky Oil building like their dads did? Was he in Calgary at the head office? Or was he away working a rig somewhere? Is that why he was never in church, even for Midnight Mass? Christopher held that candle with its paper wrapping to catch the wax and wished for the other kids to stop asking questions.

When Christopher started high school, suddenly the things that had set him apart from his peers were cool. Other kids were missing fathers, from some oil patch related accidents and the occasional re-marriage after divorce, but Chris's dad had most likely committed suicide on the highway in front of where they had built the Canadian Tire. Everyone wanted to be friends with Chris; being black—half-black (but the half didn't mean anything in town)—was different, exotic, danger-ous but still safe because Chris had gone to kindergarten with them. And all the kids walking through the halls of the high school wanted to feel like they were cool too.

Girls competed for the chance to spend Fridays and Saturdays wherever Chris was planning on being. Dads, moms, ex-boy-friends, catty girlfriends, even the priest who had an accent like Arnold Schwarzenegger, everyone noticed who Chris dated. There wasn't really any jealousy among the gaggle of girls Chris let go. He never stayed with one long enough for them to feel especially important. And it was exposure that mattered to them more than anything Chris could give them.

Chris appreciated his friends and he liked popularity. Being popular felt good and it seemed to calm his mother. She asked fewer questions about what his day was like, preferring to ask about one of his friends from school or hockey, or one of his girlfriends. Their names were comforting. Still, when Chris came home at night and unlocked the door to his house, kicked off his shoes in the front hall and made his way to his basement bedroom, he was sure this change had nothing to do with the town accepting him into the fold. It was something else. Like a rare stamp being added to a collection.

Chris's mom was at work, so he didn't think twice about turning his stereo system up loud so late. He sang along as he stripped off his oversized jeans and threw his Oilers jersey into a corner with his other dirty laundry. No one, none of his friends from school or their younger siblings who gossiped to their friends that Christopher Brant had been over to play PlayStation at their house last night, would believe Chris if he told them that his favourite album wasn't hip hop, rap, or even rock, but something by Michael Bublé.

PUPPY DOWN

T HE BELL SIGNALLING THE END OF LUNCH had rung and most of the Grade 12 students filed into Christian Ethics class, their bellies full and their minds foggy. Poppy sat with her back held straight in the second row. She was chatting with a girlfriend, laughing at something her friend said, but she was facing the front of the room, even though the teacher was still hovering over her desk waiting for stragglers.

Chuck slipped in through the door and took a seat at the back of the room in his usual place. He didn't have a backpack, a textbook or a pen. But he was there. Almost on time, too.

His sister didn't turn around. She stiffened in her chair as if she could feel his presence in the room. Bill would make his way up to the desk next to Poppy's, sit next to her while the teacher tried to engage the students in a discussion about the Israelites, early Christian history, or her favourite topic, miracles. Poppy reached out to brush old eraser crumbs from Bill's desk, preferring to keep the surface clean of debris, and waited for him.

I I I I

BETWEEN FIFTH AND SIXTH PERIOD, Poppy cornered her brother. A young teacher, his lip covered by a thin mustache, stood in the doorway watching them. Chuck answered her under his breath. "I haven't seen Billy-boy. Not since lunch. He wasn't feeling one hundred percent and took an opportunity to lounge in front of the TV for the afternoon."

"Oh," Poppy replied.

But Poppy was nervous, sweaty, turning on her cellphone before she made it to the front doors. She drove to work with her phone tucked between her knees so she could feel it ring over her car stereo's bass. Her phone was typically abandoned in the back room during her shift. At work, Poppy found herself covered in flour and pizza sauce, and that kind of stuff gummed up the keys. But today she kept her phone in her apron pocket inside a zip-lock bag, waiting for him to call and maybe tell her that he was doing alright, had watched a Discovery program about sharks.

I I I I

IN THE MORNING, with telltale shadows under her eyes, Poppy made it to homeroom just as the bell rang. Chuck was already in his seat, spinning his pencil from finger to finger like an acrobat. The teacher, a plump married woman who sang terribly off-key in church, stood at the front of the room. Her hands were tucked into the pockets of her blazer. Bill still wasn't in his chair.

"I have some news. Settle down," their teacher said more firmly when the early morning chatter did not subside. "Our classmate Bill is away today."

Chuck's pencil stopped spinning, slipped to the ground. Poppy turned and stared at her brother as if whatever was about to happen was Chuck's fault because he had lunch with Bill yesterday before Bill started feeling sick. The pencil settled on the ground and Chuck ignored it, knowing with the look in their teacher's eye, that he wouldn't need a pencil today. They'd be discussing miracles again.

"Bill's in the hospital. And will be for the rest of the week. For observation. His mother thought that you all should know. We'll pray for his health today."

"What's wrong with him?"

"Well, that's up to Bill to say, if he wants to, when he returns, Charles." She let her announcement sit in the room for a minute before instructing the class to pull out their agendas. Chuck bent over to retrieve his pencil from the floor.

I I I I

LATER, THE BELL RINGING, the lunch period concluded for another day, Chuck came running down the hallway. "Shit, Poppy," he hollered. Several students and a teacher turned to stare.

"Language, Lansing!"

"Shit!" Chuck said. "God forsaken shit." He rubbed his unshaven face nervously, turned around and attacked the wall of lockers with his fists. Then exploded, kicking and punching the lockers. The teacher and students watched quietly. When Chuck got up close to his sister, he pulled at her sleeve. "I made him sick."

"How?" Poppy crossed her arms over her chest, distancing herself from her brother. Her heart thumping, knowing that this had been someone's fault.

"I made him order…too much. Two animal burgers, a fucking milkshake and fries with mayo." Chuck looked at her, realizing that he hadn't really given his sister enough information. "He's got diabetes."

"He's okay?" Her voice sounded detached, even to Poppy.

"He's fine. His parents won't let him have his phone. He needs his rest," Chuck said in a voice that mocked Bill's mother's faint British accent.

"Oh. That's okay."

"You're not listening." His voice rose, but he settled down when it looked as if the teacher in the hallway was about to intervene. "It's all my fault."

Before Poppy could tell her brother how dumb he really was, their Christian Ethics teacher poked her head out into the hallway and said, "Jesus is waiting!"

"You would like it if you were cancerous, wouldn't you Chuck? Then you could blame yourself for everything and not have to deal with reality. It's so much easier if you're the fuckup, isn't it?" Poppy yelled at her brother as she walked through the classroom doorway.

Chuck made to follow her, but his Christian Ethics teacher stopped him. "Maybe it would be wise to take the day off, Charles."

She wasn't giving him an option. Chuck decided to meet his cousin at the Holiday Inn for a drink after all. He would make it up to Bill as soon as Bill was feeling better.

AFTER SCHOOL SPECIAL

T HE CONSTRUCTION SITE beside the Catholic high school was not fenced off and students who lived in the older housing district beyond the broken ground often walked through the site after school. Plastic water main tubes the colour of glacier runoff water and segments of immense concrete pipeline which were to be buried underground lay in the dirt lined up along a newly paved street. After school, after family dinners, after punching out of the after school job, Lillian and her friends would pile into cars wearing their chunky knit sweaters, bought *en masse* during a sale at the mall. They might stop for takeout coffee spiked with low-calorie sweeteners before they drove to the construction site.

The girls climbed into one of the concrete tubes and sat down with their coffees in hand for another exciting Friday night. They giggled and sipped at the coffee that they didn't really like but figured made them seem more grown-up than hot chocolate or a can of pop. They complained about the weather starting to turn. They fell silent. Lillian checked her cellphone. It was quarter after nine.

"What should we do?"

"No clue."

Lillian said, "It's always the same thing—"

"There's that party?"

"That's a bad idea," Lillian said. "Really bad. You know how those things go. Everyone drives home drunk."

"We won't be drinking, Lillian. Just having a little fun."

"Obviously." Jenna echoed the sentiment.

"Lillian, it's just something to do."

Outvoted, Lillian considered going straight home. But since she was driving tonight, it would have caused all kinds of unnecessary drama. None of the girls would have said they were mad—they were too grown-up for that kind of nonsense—but there would have been arms firmly crossed and dark silences while they pretended to listen to every word of the commercials on the radio. They all would have argued it was their turn to be let off first.

Lillian drove out of town, following the highway toward Saskatoon. Just past the lights at the Husky Upgrader station, Lillian turned left onto a side road that soon faded to gravel. She slowed down, saying something about bald tires and dirt that hadn't been packed down in a while. She watched the speedometer falling and felt better.

From the backseat, Jenna's cellphone glowed. "It's further down. Off the road, past the field."

Lillian could smell the bonfire before she saw the cars parked in the pasture next to the trees on someone's dad's farm. She parked next to a pickup she didn't recognize. The girls climbed out of the car and began migrating towards the sounds of the party, country music, boys laughing, girls squealing and travelling in packs.

Lillian stuck close to her friends with an arm tucked into the crook of the closest elbow. She wanted to find someone she knew, someone who wasn't too drunk and might just want to talk, calmly, about something like school or the weather. The first person she recognized was her brother, a can in one hand, a cigarette in the other, Cory standing next to him.

She turned away, pulled her arm from the safety of her friend's and began to walk, in slow, measured steps back to her car. She would wait there, clean the dust off the dashboard with her fingers in the moonlight. Recline the seat and cover herself with her coat. Maybe sleep if she didn't get too cold.

His voice came from behind her, but it was close enough to startle her. "Lillian! Your brother says you never come out."

"Yeah," she said. Turned to face Cory. "I would much rather be somewhere else."

76

Cory laughed. "Why did you come? I mean, why do something you clearly, really, definitely don't want to be doing?"

"Peer pressure," she said and Cory smiled. "That and you know…"

"Yeah," he said, but the tone of his voice said that he didn't really know. He was busy playing his part humouring a pretty girl at a party in the prairie bush on a dirty corner of some cow field.

"There's really nothing else to do."

Cory was the kind of guy who enjoyed a girl who knew exactly what she didn't like.

THE LAST FLIGHT BEFORE THE STORM

MIKE LEFT GLOSSY VACATION INSERTS found in the newspaper, inserts with three folds and the ocean always pictured in colours Mike had only seen in the expensive paints at the hardware store, on his wife's bedside table. He had dog-eared the corners of a few packages to sun destinations if they had yoga studios looking out over the ocean. Not that Barb did yoga. But she might, he thought, if she could do yoga next to the ocean and not in their cramped living room, next to the fireplace and the TV. In the inserts, bamboo huts shielded smiling, tanned and buff men and women from the sun, smoothie and juice bars lingered in the background to refresh them afterwards. Mike let news of his co-workers' upcoming holidays slip into conversations during dinner or at the supermarket in the produce aisle. Barb would nod as she tried to listen to the softly playing radio or to the voice overhead announcing spills in the adjacent aisle.

Mike left a blank vacation request form on the kitchen counter next to his wife's coffee machine for three weeks. Every day she cleaned and replaced the filter, exchanged one coffee mug for another. It was as if his wife hadn't seen the form sitting there. But Mike had found a coffee-stained fingerprint in the left hand corner, wrinkling the paper.

He circled a week on the family-sized calendar with the pen that had been clipped onto it ever since the day Poppy complained in a violent teenage rage that she could never find a pen in their goddamned house. The pen lingered there even though Mike and Barb knew very well where other pens were kept. But Poppy knew where the junk drawer was too, the day she'd made the pen stand in for whatever it was that had torn into her. Staring at that pen, Mike picked up the phone and called the travel agency in the mall. He booked two tickets for a week in a fancy resort hotel with a room looking out over the Caribbean Sea. The agent didn't have to work hard to convince Mike to upgrade to the couples package. Bottles of nice wine every night, strawberries and chocolate to dip them in upon check-in, a voucher for his and hers massages, and a guaranteed room with private Jacuzzi tub and a shower with a view of the salt water pool.

It was no secret that Mike had booked their holiday. He left the credit card statement on top of his wife's Sudoku book; he wrote the flight information on the calendar in his neatest handwriting; he started packing, gathering his little-used swim trunks and a bottle of expired sun cream from the medicine cabinet and laying them out on their bed. She had to move the items from the bed to the floor before she could go to sleep at night. She had to touch them and think about throwing out the expired sun cream every night.

The day before their flight was scheduled to take off, the weatherman was predicting a storm, wearing a green Roughriders winter toque, and a scarf to illustrate his point. Heavy snow, poor driving conditions, dangerously low wind chill, the kind of weather that Mike was used to witnessing from the comfort of his living room with his electric fireplace glowing. Flights were already being cancelled in anticipation, but Mike finished packing and carried his suitcase out to the truck. He turned the key to let the engine warm up while he went back into the house to advise his wife of their imminent departure.

"We had better get going if we want to outrun this storm." Mike stood in their hallway, the wet snow heavy on his shoulders. The puddles beginning to form in the lobby under his feet were laced with mud.

Barb was sitting at the kitchen table, sorting through next week's flyers. She'd already trashed the vacation inserts and the flyers for the electronics store.

"Did you hear me?"

"I'm not sure you've been hearing me."

"There's a storm coming. I don't want to end up driving in it."

"I know."

"Okay," he said. Mike stomped his winter boots on the mat, letting the flecks of dirty sleet settle there, thankful that he wouldn't have to wear the boots much longer.

PAROLE DREAMS

CHUCK KEPT HIMSELF BUSY dealing with the things in his head for most of the first year after he checked into the federal detention centre. Simmering in his cell, time slowly evaporating, he became bored with thinking about how he found himself here. He started to consider what his days would be like after this was over. Life after Chuck was done serving the time that the courts deemed long enough to atone for his part in an idealistic, youthful, wispy-haired boy's death. No matter how he tried, Chuck could not envision a life that didn't include Bill riding shotgun in Chuck's truck.

News had come that Chuck's cellmate, Rickie, had been granted parole after three years living in a six-by-eight-foot room. As a young man who didn't know any better and found that making money was easier if he did it by stealing flat screen TVs or Kitchenaid stand mixers rather than through a conventional job, Rickie wound up paying in years, an uneven exchange. But Rickie was walking out with a few hundred dollars and a certificate in Animal Husbandry. He could get a job on a farm somewhere. Maybe his ex-wife would take him back and Rickie could escort his daughters to school before he drove out to the dairy farm and began working with dappled cows. Maybe he could buy his ex-wife a KitchenAid stand mixer at a department store this time around.

Chuck paced around the perimeter of the exercise yard, while Rickie visited with his daughters inside, breaking the good news to them in person. Chuck had never wanted kids of his own, or a Kitchenaid stand mixer, or a wife to blame his financial problems on when the stand mixer went unused for years, collecting dust on his kitchen counter. When he was outside, he passed off diapered cousins to his father or sister and picked up one of his uncles' unwatched beers. On his release, Chuck would be too old to start a family, he figured. Even if he could convince a good woman to marry him, mate and incubate his child, then show him how to parent it. She'd have to be the kind who might possibly make up for his deficiencies as a person. She'd have to be younger than him, so that she would be alive to see their kid through university. The best he could hope for was to be released and find a job where he could make enough money for a woman with kids already partly grown to be attracted to his stability. She'd have to have grown up far away from Chuck's hometown. To her Bill could be a story, a sad story told in the past tense.

The oil sands might hire Chuck when he got out. They did background checks on the men that worked on the rigs, but only so they knew what they were dealing with. They didn't necessarily weed out men who had done time for falling on the wrong side of the law. Chuck could make handfuls of money working long, dirty hours.

Or Chuck could go the way Rickie had and get a career. Rickie had told him that the government axed the program to educate federal prisoners a long time ago. Too costly. Too soft and liberal. Too many angry citizens being interviewed on television about toughening up prison sentences, eliminating indulgences, punishing convicted criminals properly. But if Chuck could get a hold of a little money, from his family, from a kind, doting uncle, Chuck could pay for it himself, like Rickie had. Chuck would have to apply and be accepted on his own merit. Chuck would have to ask his family for help. He couldn't see a day where he could bring himself to do that, though. And Chuck knew he didn't have a way with animals.

Rickie had promised to come and visit Chuck on occasion, to keep him in the loop on the goings-on outside. While that sounded like it might be welcome, seeing someone he knew, Chuck supposed in all probability it would never happen.

When they let Chuck out, he wouldn't be coming back.

LONG-TERM PARKING

MIKE PARKED HIS TRUCK in long-term parking. He abandoned his parka in the back seat of his cab and walked with his shoulders braced straight into the storm battering Saskatoon. Planes were still taking off. Mike could see their headlights bisecting the snow as he made his way to the terminal along an unplowed walkway in a pair of shoes better suited for walking in Bud Miller All Seasons Park in June.

Mike's plane waited on the runway for hours as the de-icer made its rounds. Other passengers were complaining about the delay, but Mike had his eyes closed and his neck open and exposed. With the vents pumping out a steady stream of hot air, it was as if he was already getting closer to the centre of the world. He could taste salt on his lips. Even though he thought he wouldn't like it, Mike was going to try yoga. The boys in the office would get a kick out of it. So would the secretaries.

At the hotel, Mike approached the tanned, dark-haired receptionist, cleared his throat of the leftover Canadian cold and upgraded his couples hotel package for a nicer room, a premium mattress and a panoramic view of the ocean from the bathroom. The bed was as wide as it was long and the mattress reminded Mike of a marshmallow. He peeled back the sheets to study the construction of the mattress top. It was still white, despite the numerous bodies that had slept on it, that had romped on it. The receptionist with the dark hair told Mike this room was one of their top sellers with the German tourist set.

Mike hoped the German tourists slept better than he did on the marshmallow mattress. He rose earlier than he would have at home, hoping a shower would ease the pain in his back. At eight a.m., he decided to go to the beach. After only a few hours, Mike was burnt so badly his skin felt as if it were shrinking at an alarming rate. A corresponding tightening of the muscles in his chest got Mike thinking about skin cancer and the four-hour wait to get a chance to try out one of the motorized water scooters advertised in the brochure. A boy of about sixteen kicked up the sand as he weaved through the plastic sun-chairs peddling weak, rum-based, fluorescent coloured drinks on a tight schedule. Other than the hint of an early mustache, this kid could be his own son, when Chuck had been fifteen, on a competitive soccer team, the year before Chuck stopped playing soccer altogether. Mike thought that the boy kept better time than a game clock and that his gaudy orange hotel shirt was too loose when the orange jersey Mike had bought for his fifteen-year-old son the last year he played had fit so well.

Relinquishing his seat in the sun, Mike strolled out onto the strip of shops, restaurants and Starbucks extending as far as he could see between the resorts and length of the ocean. In real life, it wasn't as blue. When it was time for lunch, Mike didn't want to eat at the five-star Japanese restaurant conveniently located in the lobby of his hotel or at the poolside American Bar and Grill. He wanted to taste Mexico, to eat food fried along with a handful of habaneros, to smell the char on corn tortillas like the kind he had seen on a Mayan PBS special. Was there a beer he could taste that wasn't served with an eighth of a lime?

So he walked past the upscale boutiques selling swimming suits adorned with crystals and American chain restaurants' neon signs. As he wandered further down the strip, the resort hotels became smaller, and the white and yellow coloured buildings near him were in need of a pressure washing to peel away the silt clinging to their walls. Several taxi drivers stopped to ask if Mike was lost, wandering so far away from the resorts, his sunburnt skin like a beacon. Mike waved them all away.

For a while nothing but shrubs lined the road and when the shrubs cleared, a dirt path leading down to a public beach was announced only by a sign. *Playa Caracol.* A bus ambled past Mike, leaving the smell of diesel in the air. An orange-uniformed woman leaned against the bus window, a few other hotel uniforms visible as the bus passed Mike on the shoulder. *Playa Tortuga. Playa Langosta.* Then *Playa Linda.* If it weren't for the sharp hunger pain in his stomach rivaling the sunburn, Mike would have wandered down one of the paths to examine the beaches where a Mexican family might come for the day. Where two kids might play in the froth of the salted water. Running along the length of the beach, trying to rub handfuls of sand in each other's hair as they screamed with mock fear, with glee. A boy and his little sister. When the next bus passed Mike, he flagged it down.

❚ ❚ ❚

TWO WEEKS AFTER MIKE LANSING'S SCHEDULED RETURN, a Saskatoon Airport Authority parking official billed his credit card for the extended stay, and found that the card had been cancelled. Sighing, the parking official, reeling from a bad hangover, used a wire hanger to help himself to the winter coat before he contacted a tow truck. Collateral damage. The parking official was proud that he only scratched the paint on the truck once.

RIGHT BEHIND YOU

POPPY COULD PROBABLY CROSS THE BORDER into Mexico, slip across some sleepy border town and not be noticed by either country. Not missed, either. If she found the right spot, avoided army trucks loaded with men and machine guns. But she would never get into America overland and there would be no flying until her official documents were kosher. Getting a passport replaced in a foreign country was among the list of things that Poppy never really wanted to experience in her life, falling somewhere between suffering on prom night from the pain of a really nasty hangnail, the kind that bled all over the place when it was picked, and being in love with a dead boy.

Not that Poppy had been thinking about going back yet, but now she was. Poppy opened the door and stepped out onto the street for the first time that day. Was there a black market for Canadian passports taking payment by overdrawn credit card? She supposed that was as unlikely as the passport thief tracking her down to return her document, asking her to lunch to repay the emotional hardship of his crime.

She glanced down the street looking for signs of the dog. He might be lying with his head between his paws in the recessed doorway of a shop, or standing perfectly still mid-street, ears perky, tail drooping to the ground. Even if Poppy couldn't spot him, she was sure he was just off beyond the things she could see. In her mind, she saw his rib bones strain against wisps of blond fur.

Walking down the street in the direction of the water, Poppy heard the click of the dog's nails on the cobblestones. If she turned around, he would stop, hesitating a few metres behind her like a shadow. He never got close enough for her to reach out and touch him. Whenever she left her little apartment to wander through the city, listlessly trying to decide if she should pack and make her way to the bus station, Poppy had the feeling that if she turned around very quickly, she would be able to see something that she could not put into words. But when she turned around, it was always just the big-eared dog.

"You should not feed them," the street vendor told her, the day she ordered three pieces of fried chicken. Poppy threw two pieces of breaded meat out into the street almost as soon as the vendor took them from under the orange glow of a heat lamp. "¡Basta! Why do you feed him?"

Both Poppy and the street vendor then admired how the dog kept the other dogs back with a low growl, how the dog managed to growl as he ate the greasy chicken.

The bus station was on the far side of town. Poppy had a strong inclination to turn around. Change directions, head towards the terminal. Catch purpose with her hands and swallow it whole. Poppy wanted to absorb this feeling like the paper towels her mother touted whenever her husband, son or one of the rotating dinner guests knocked a glass with their elbow. But if Poppy turned around too quickly, the feeling that had set in told her she would never come back here. She might never go anywhere again.

She roamed the river heading north. She stopped at an empty tourist lookout where she could observe local families swimming in the shallows, pulling fishing boats out onto the sand. One of the kids standing knee-deep in the water saw her watching and mimed for Poppy to take photographs of him. He jumped up and down saying, "Photo, photo!" The rest of the family turned to stare.

Time to leave. Poppy turned around and catching sight of someone she had left behind her so long ago now, inhaled sharply.

"Hello," Juan-Aarón said. "How are you, my flower, my love?" At her silence, he continued, "I was holding your passport for you for safekeeping. You forgot to ask for it when you left."

Poppy looked away from Juan-Aarón to see if the dog was close by. He was tucked against the stone wall dividing the walkway from the beach below. The local boy had stopped yelling for his picture to be taken. It was very quiet in the bright sunlight.

"You did not say goodbye. I purchased two tickets for the ocean busliner. Expensive bottles of water you liked because they contained the bubbles. What did I do wrong?"

The dog began whimpering.

"Could I have it back? Now. Please," Poppy said. She kept her arms firmly at her sides. Her nails were long and she could use them if she had to, long enough for the locals to come to her aid.

Juan-Aarón looked so sad, with his scar running through his lip.

"I was following... Remember I told you about that...ghost. I was following him."

Juan-Aarón exhaled heavily. "Oh. Okay. That makes sense." He looked down at his boots, then quickly again up at Poppy. "Um, do you see him now?" He reached into his breast pocket, held the passport out to Poppy. He was sad when American girls were sick like this, broken like this.

She took it. "No."

"Okay then. I, well, wanted to say farewell to you. It has been interesting."

Poppy watched him walk away, her palms sweaty and warm, feeling as if she had been dumped. "Come on, dog." There was no need to look to see if he was following her.

HOLES IN THE DRYWALL

FRANK CAME OVER TO THE HOUSE every day after he was done work. Sometimes he might not come over until well after ten, sometimes he could be found applying a fresh coat of stain to the deck before Barb extracted herself from bed in the mornings. Since Mike had left for his mid-winter vacation, Frank had been there every step of the way, dropping by to eat leftovers and to reassure Barb between bites that in all likelihood, Mike was probably not having an affair. It was just a vacation.

When Barb got the call that Mike's truck was being towed from the airport in Saskatoon to an impound lot, it was Frank who paid for the gas to go out and hook up his best friend's truck so he could bring it home. The truck waited in the drive-way of Mike and Barb's house for someone to drive it. Barb had always refused to get behind the wheel of the truck, preferring her Civic's sensible seats and turn radius.

"I could go back to the beauty counter. They would only pay minimum wage, but at least it would be something."

Frank nodded noncommittally.

"I had to cancel the cable last week, Frank!"

Barb was one of the few people Frank knew who didn't schedule her evenings around prime time. She finally ordered cable in the late nineties as a Christmas gift for the kids. Frank took that into consideration before he spoke, using the tone he reserved for strange dogs chained up in the back of pickup trucks he had been sent to repossess: "You're going to have to sell the house."

She refilled her coffee mug, laughing awkwardly. "Do you know, Frank? How low I've gone? Last week, I checked to see what I would have to do to cash in his life insurance policy." Returning to join Frank at the table, she laughed louder. "Seven years. I have to wait seven years before I can claim the money to pay the mortgage. All because I can't prove that he's dead."

"I don't believe he's dead. Not with one fibre of my being. Neither do you."

"If I thought he were dead, I would never have bothered cancelling the cable. Poppy used to like watching the specialty movie channels." She moved a few things around on the table, just to do something with her hands. "I'd have just found some way to prove he was dead."

They fell quiet and Frank sipped his coffee. His cellphone rang and he went to press the ignore button, but Barb answered it for him. "Sure, he'll be right over." She pushed the phone across the table. "Accident just past the old bingo hall."

▮ ▮ ▮ ▮

BARB DIDN'T CALL FRANK FOR OVER A WEEK. She snubbed him in the Safeway, pushing her cart right past his without more than a nod of acknowledgement. He figured she needed some thinking space after he suggested she sell. Maybe he should have started with the idea of subletting while she visited her sister for a few months.

But on Sunday, the phone rang. "Would you help me get the house in shape," Barb asked. "I've already talked to Katy Smith, Helen Smith's sister, at RE/MAX."

Because he was a good man, Frank showed up with his toolbox and began to turn the Lansing's family home into something that Barb could sell. He helped tear up the carpet in Chuck's old room because it had a bad smell, fixed leaky faucets and greased the track the garage door sat on. That squeak had always bothered Frank. When it looked like the house was finally ready for a showing, on a last whim, Frank lifted a family portrait from the wall for a perfunctory dusting unveiling a large hole in the drywall.

"Barb? You have any other holes you want me to patch up?

'Cause it would be easier if you just tell me where they are."

She emerged from the master bedroom, "Actually, no. I don't."

"You sure about that? This is an easy fix. A few layers of putty, sanding—"

"Nobody gets a perfect house. Put the picture back."

Frank wasn't quite sure how to respond. So he carried the frame to the sink, wiped it down with a dishcloth and returned the picture to its place on the wall. The streaks on the glass from Frank's effort at cleaning didn't bother Barb like she thought they would.

"When you leave," she asked, lugging a box out of the bedroom, "would you take this? Keep it. Drop it off at the dump, whatever."

"Of course. Yeah."

"Thanks for helping with—you know—the house."

"It's... You're welcome. You're family."

When Frank was ready to leave, he gathered his tools and sat down on the steps in the entranceway to lace up his boots. He didn't peer into the open box until he was carrying it outside. He was now the proud owner of a couple dozen bottles of unopened wine, the kind the Lansings served at Sunday dinners, and the contents of the male side of a medicine cabinet.

THOSE IS FIGHTING WORDS

C HRISTOPHER SAT WITH HIS LEGS DANGLING off the stretcher. The curtain had been pulled around the bed for privacy. Surgery green, Sergeant W. Leroy thought. "Surgery green," Leroy said to the boy sitting on the stretcher. Leroy had one foot on the seat of an old swivel chair. He used his knee as a makeshift table and was taking notes when Erin ripped open the curtain.

"Who the hell did this to you?"

Chris took his hand away from the bandages covering his nose. "Bikers."

"Your son," Leroy said, "got into a fistfight in the bar off of the Yellowhead on the Saskatchewan side."

"My son was in a bar?" she asked, without waiting for a reply. "My son was in a bar. Christopher, you were in a bar? You're fifteen, Christopher. Fifteen!" Erin stepped inside the half-open curtain, pulled it closed behind her and moved to sit next to her son. "Are you...okay?"

"I busted my nose."

"They told me that. I mean, are *you* okay?"

"Yeah," Chris said.

"So what happened?" Erin asked, looking from her son to Leroy. "Do you have the people who did this in custody?" Erin ran her fingers through her son's tightly braided hair.

"Yes, but once Christopher is released, I'm going to have to take him down to the station for follow-up. The reports take time."

Christopher kicked the stretcher, dislodging his mother's hand. "He called me a... You know."

"He did what?" Erin asked, then realized what her son meant. "Oh Chris. I'm sorry."

"The worst was he asked me which one of the town whores was my mother." Christopher fell silent, looked down at his shoes, which were stained with his own blood. "So I hit him," Chris said with renewed vigor. "And then he hit me back. Why do noses bleed so much mom?"

"The owner called the cops when your boy went down," Leroy said.

Erin sighed. "Let me see if we can get him out of here."

The next day, a little before noon, when Christopher wandered up the stairs, he saw Erin sitting at the kitchen table typing on his laptop. She didn't ask him why he had skipped school today; she hadn't woken him either, as she lay in bed watching the neon lights of her alarm clock.

"Do you want some breakfast?"

"Just juice." Christopher opened the fridge and pulled out the orange juice carton. His cellphone lit up. Quickly, Chris pressed the ignore button, sending the call to voice mail.

Before her son could join her at the table, Erin announced, "I'm looking for a new job. In Saskatoon."

"I think that's a good idea."

"I was saving up to buy you a car for your birthday, but I think I've changed my mind."

"That's okay."

Erin reached for the extra glass her son had carried with him to the table, his finger crooked inside the glass. She helped herself to some orange juice. "Why did you pick that bar?"

Chris smiled. "You're not letting this go, are you?"

"Nope." Erin was smiling too.

"We heard we probably wouldn't get ID'd."

Erin snorted. "That's because you picked the seediest bar in town. Now go get yourself dressed, I'm taking you to school. You'll be just in time for Christian Ethics."

Downstairs in his room, Christopher dialed his voice mail. Thirty-six new messages, the computerized voice said. Chris was more popular than ever.

ALLEGIANCES

L ILLIAN LEANED OUT OF THE TAKEOUT WINDOW. The sweet smell of her brother's favourite indulgence stung her nose. "I can't."

"Won't is the word you were looking for," Lillian's brother said, slumped down in his car's bucket seat. Cory was next to him, his eyes hidden under a baseball cap advertising for a Toronto team.

"Fine, I won't give you free coffee or free sandwiches. Not even day-old donuts. We throw those out."

"Why not Lillian? I'm family," her brother taunted. "Moral objections? Scared your boss, the big man upstairs, or Daddy is watching?"

Lillian without censoring herself said exactly what she was thinking, "Because you deal drugs. I don't associate with scum like drug dealers. Even if they are related to me."

Lillian's brother cracked up. It was deep laughter, coming straight from the gut, the kind where it's possible for a little urine to escape in the process. "Do you know how crazy you are?" he managed to get out between fits.

Cory watched Lillian covertly from under his hat, feeling bad for her.

When Lillian's brother sobered up, he said, "Everyone who smokes is dealing crystal and heroin, aren't they, Lily? You're so naïve, eager to listen to what everyone says. Can't think with your own pretty head." Lillian's brother revved his engine. Behind him in the drive-through line, a car honked with impatience. "Why don't you—"

Lillian didn't hear her brother's parting shot. His tires squealed, burning rubber. Closing the takeout window manually, she began rearranging things on the counter; she moved a nearly empty coffee pot from one percolator to another, turning off the one closest to the drive-through window, wiped the counter down with a yellowing J-cloth and was considering how many boxes of cups to bring up from the storage room, feeling almost proud when Cory walked into the empty store.

"I would really like a coffee," Cory said. "I'm even willing to pay for it." He smiled. "Yeah, I want to pay for it."

"For one of my brother's friends, that's unusual. A regular coffee?"

"Double-double," he said. Fishing his wallet out of his jeans, he asked, "What would it take to get a job here?"

"An application. Not coming in here high. That would help."

"I didn't—"

Lillian smiled sharply and Cory stopped in mid-sentence. She held up the regular sized coffee cup.

Cory nodded. "I didn't smoke. I don't smoke. I was just in the car."

"Coffee. A dollar thirty-eight." She placed it on the counter in front of herself, instead of pushing it across to the patron like the training video had instructed her to.

He pulled a twenty out his wallet, a homemade silver duct-taped creation, starting to come apart at the folded seam. "Hey Lillian, what are you doing Saturday?"

When she took the bill from his hand, he touched her palm with his thumb. "Nothing." She shrugged. "Maybe working if they need a shift covered." Crossed her arms tightly over her breasts. "Homework." Uncrossed them. "I'll get your change."

"Would you rather have dinner with me? At my dad's girlfriend's place? It's out a ways, but I can drive us, no problem."

Lillian fought to keep her eyebrows neutral. "Isn't that the night you usually hang with my brother and his friends playing cards in my basement? You know, drinking beer."

"You forgot the PlayStation."

She laughed and a car in the parking lot laid on its horn twice.

Long and sharp, like when Lillian's brother used to have to drive her to ballet before she finally secured her learner's permit.

"It's my birthday."

She handed him back his twenty, cleared the purchase from her till. "Okay."

The horn again.

"I want to make some changes. Can I start by calling you Lily?"

"If you want."

At dinner on Saturday, three of them sat around the kitchen table waiting for the phone to ring. They had eaten pizza off of napkins so that nobody would have to do the dishes. Although they weren't supposed to eat pizza at all. It was a last minute substitution for a home cooked meal. A birthday could not trump a company emergency in Fort McMurray.

"Room for cake?" Cory's dad's girlfriend asked, breaking the silence. She threw her long braid over her shoulder, out of the way. "I picked it up at the Safeway. The best looking one. With real sugary icing. Sorry about the pink. It was the best looking one."

"No. Thanks, not right this minute," Cory said. "Lily, do you want to come out to the barn and see the car I've been working on?"

Outside in the chill of the evening, Cory led Lily around the barn, showing her the car, where he'd sanded away rust, parts of the engine laid out on strips of cardboard to soak up the grease. Sitting on old bales of hay smelling of mould, they talked about what colour Cory should paint the car. Cory heard the phone ring, he heard his dad's girlfriend call out the front door, but he made his first adult decision and stayed outside with a pretty girl who had her head screwed on right, and a car that could one day hold its own in town.

I I I I

PERMISSIONS

ACKNOWLEDGEMENTS

Portions of *Border Markers* have appeared in *Festival Writer*. Much thanks to Jane Carman for all she does to support writers.

My time at the University of Windsor shaped this book—and many of my thoughts about writing. A very big thank you to Susan Holbrook for inviting me to her office on Thursday, Friday, and even the occasional Saturday afternoon, for her encouraging words, and for writing *Good Egg Bad Seed* (which I adore and which you should read). Thanks to Dale Jacobs for leaving a copy of *How I Became a Famous Novelist* on my desk. Humour always helps when the writing times are tough. Thanks to Nicholas Papador for giving me a lot to think about when it comes to the tempo of my writing. Thanks to Maria Bastien, Hollie Adams (*Things You've Inherited From Your Mother*), Ava Homa (*Echoes from the Other Land*), and James Farrington for friendship and feedback. If Louis Cabri hadn't given me a gentle push in the opposite direction of where I had been running, *Border Markers* would be a lumbering 400-page novel. You may thank him for this.

Lloydminster, thank you. For then, and for now, Kalie, Kelly, Fallon, Sheila, Nicole, I raise a glass.

Thanks to Callie, Tanya, and Pinky for all the years; to Rickie Ann, Sara, and Val for the hard years; to the whole Pitch Wars #15 crew (but especially to Anne Lipton, Tracy Gold, and Alivya Leighton), thank you, and here's to the years to come.

Thanks to Holly Baker—she knows why.

Thanks to the team at NeWest and my editor Anne Nothof for believing in this book.

Of course, a million thanks to my sisters, parents, aunts, and uncles, and grandpa for making me feel like what I do is impressive.

And thank you, dear reader. Books change people, and by changing people, they change the world. Here's to readers, books, and change.

Montréal-born Jenny Ferguson is a writer, editor and teacher who lives in a log cabin (without an internet connection) and names her pets after (dead) American presidents. She holds a PhD in English from the University of South Dakota. You can reach her at jennyferguson.ca.